A Meeting on the Andheri Overbridge

A Meeting on the Andheri Overbridge

Sudha Gupta Investigates

Ambai

Translated by
Gita Subramanian

JUGGERNAUT BOOKS
KS House, 118 Shahpur Jat, New Delhi 110049, India

First published in Tamil as *Andheri Membalathil Oru Santhippu: Sudha Guptavin Thuppariyum Anubavangal*
by Kalachuvadu Publications 2014
First published by Juggernaut Books 2016

Copyright © Ambai 2016
Translation copyright © Gita Subramanian 2016

10 9 8 7 6 5 4 3 2 1

All rights reserved. No part of this publication may be reproduced, transmitted, or stored in a retrieval system in any form or by any means without the written permission of the publisher.

For sale in the Indian Subcontinent only

ISBN 9788193284193

Typeset in Adobe Caslon Pro by R. Ajith Kumar, New Delhi

Printed and bound at Thomson Press India Ltd

Contents

As the Day Darkens	1
The Paperboat Maker	95
A Meeting on the Andheri Overbridge	141
A Note on the Author	199
A Note on the Translator	201

As the Day Darkens

Sounds of laughter as they began to play. A small plastic bucket, a spade and such came out of their bags. All three began to sing 'Barah mahine mein bara tareekese tujhko pyaar jataavunga re...Dhinka chika dhinka chika...' *and began to dig a hole in the sand. A large pit deep enough to hide in – their plan was, when the waves rushed in and their hole filled with water, they would jump in and play. All three busied themselves shovelling very fast but at the same time they jumped around flinging sand at each other, leaping up and thumping each other on the back and pulling each other's plaits. Every 'dhinka chika' meant a break from the digging to dance rolling one's hips. There was no one nearby; at a great distance, a few. The Malayalee selling coconut water could be seen as a dot on the other side of the rocks.*

The orange-coloured sun had slipped into the palm fronds and begun to touch the edge of the sea. It was the time to assess the events of the day, to run them through the mind.

Stella had entered all the data into the computer, printed the reports, filed them and left for home. She had filled the electric kettle and turned it on, leaving the cinnamon teabags that Sudha liked by the side. The kettle's red light went off and the button popped out. Sudha put a teabag into a cup and poured boiling water from the kettle on to it. Cinnamon fumes rose from the cup.

On the horizon, a twisted red line. In the distance, almost like a shadow, Madh Island.

She began to read the files as she sipped her tea. As darkness fell outside, stars slowly began to appear.

The cell phone rang with the song '*Oh re manwa tu toh bawra re...*'

Govind Shelke.

'Hello Govind! *Kai zala?*' she asked him in Marathi.

'Namashkar didi!' was the reply.

'*Sanga*,' she said.

'Didi, the minister will be here any time. I am really bogged down with work. A young couple had come. The husband actually fainted here. We had to have him admitted in the Brahma Kumaris' Hospital in Andheri. He's supposed to be someone who has risen rapidly in the business world. The wife had a four-year-old boy in her arms. It seems they came as a family to Madh Island. They stayed at that hotel resort which offers a weekend holiday package.'

'A man fainted – other than that there is no complication in this matter, is there?'

'Listen didi. They've three daughters. Fourteen, twelve and ten. They've all disappeared.'

'All three of them?'

'Yes.'

'When?'

'This evening.'

'Govind, what can I do? This is work for the police – your investigative team.'

'No didi! I'm not asking you to work on it. This woman is alone with her child. Her husband's in the hospital. Her home is in Thane. She's crying and she's adamant about not going home.'

'Can't you take her to the YWCA or some such place? I know that there is a hostel for women who have had to leave home in a hurry. She can stay there for a day or two. I have the hotline number.'

'No didi. She's just not in that frame of mind. It's a rather complicated situation. Would it be a bother if she were to stay with you for the night? Are you busy?'

'No, no. Just the usual husband-suspects-the-wife-and-asks-for-surveillance-on-her sort of cases. The wife is actually a shopaholic. This afternoon she was at Shoppers Stop and bought everything from plastic spoons to shoehorns – everything that was on sale. She bought ten riding habits. They were not her size. She had four trolleys full of stuff and by the time she reached the cashier's counter, she was dripping sweat in the air-conditioned shop. She is quite obese. The bill was a whopping sixty thousand!'

'If only I could get an assignment like that, didi!'

'Teasing me, huh?'

'No didi, it's the work pressure talking. But tell me, can this lady stay with you? A small favour for me?'

'OK Govind. Send her.'

'I'll fall at your feet twice on Raksha Bandhan, didi!'

'Not enough to just fall at my feet, Govind. As your didi, I am entitled to gifts too.'

'Would I forget that? I'll send the lady with Raghav Sawant.'

'OK Govind,' Sudha said as she pressed the button to disconnect the phone. She shut the file that she had been reading. She would have to send it to the jewellery merchant the next day. He suspected that his wife was giving money to her lover. He did not seem to know or notice that the house was getting filled with all kinds of stuff. What they both needed was a good psychiatrist. Ten riding habits! What was she going to do with them? She would probably buy a horse next!

When Govind Shelke was really bogged down with work he would give her something interesting – different from her usual cases of suspicion, investigating a potential bride or groom or investigating a prospective partner in a business venture. He could not employ her officially, but he would engage her privately and, one way or the other, also arrange the money to pay her.

She was the only woman in this line of business. She had stumbled into it accidentally and it had then become her profession.

∼

Pushpa and Sudha had been inseparable friends in college. Pushpa too was from a middle-class background like her. She was from a Maharashtrian family that had been living in Dadar for a very long time. Sudha's, on the other hand, was a Tamil family living in Matunga. Pushpa, however, had rich relatives. She got gifts like foreign-manufactured jeans and handbags, and she passed on some of these to Sudha as well.

Pushpa was a good student at Ruia College. She had a very good reputation there. But she would cut the classes that were held in the afternoon. She'd leave, saying, 'My mother is not well. I have to be with her.' Her mother was apparently a chronically ill person. Though she was not bedridden, every organ of her body gave her trouble every now and then. Pushpa's two sisters were younger – eleven and six – and she had to manage everything.

That particular day was an important one. When Pushpa said she was going away in the afternoon, Sudha just could not bear it.

'But today is your birthday,' she said, looking up with a sad expression.

'Yes, that's why I have to be at home,' said Pushpa.

'Then I'll come with you.'

Pushpa opposed this vehemently. 'We live in a one-room tenement, a chawl. You will not like it there. It has a common toilet,' she said in a raised voice.

It was like a slap on her face. It felt as if Pushpa was pushing her away. Sudha quickly turned around and walked away, pretending she did not hear Pushpa's calls of 'Sudha, Sudha!'

That afternoon, however, she decided to ignore Pushpa's refusal and go to her house. If you came down from the footbridge after the Plaza Theatre and walked into the bustle of the marketplace, the building was right across the road. She bought some sweets from the corner shop and some colour pencils and colouring books for the children from the shop next to it. She walked up the wooden staircase and along the narrow corridor past the doors which had been left open to let in the breeze. The door of Pushpa's one-room house was also open. Pushpa's mother was sitting on an easy chair and picking little stones from a plate of rice. When she saw Sudha, she put the plate on the floor and got up, saying, *'Kon?'*

'I am Sudha. Pushpa's friend. Where is she?'

'She? She'll be in college now, of course! How can she be home at this time?' she said in a tone of surprise.

Sudha put everything she had in her hands on the chair close to her and said, 'I happened to be nearby. That's why I came.' She put her palms together to say namaste.

As the Day Darkens

She came out and started walking briskly towards Matunga in the hot sun.

The next day Pushpa said to her, 'I came home the moment after you had left. Why did you have to buy sweets? You really shouldn't have.'

Sudha did not answer.

'Angry?' Pushpa said in a conciliatory tone. 'I went to a relative's house before going home.'

Pushpa took Sudha's hand in hers. A pair of fine gold bangles adorned her hands.

The morning classes went on as usual. In the afternoon, Pushpa touched her on the shoulder and gestured that she had to leave. Sudha nodded in acknowledgement. But as soon as Pushpa reached the gate she stood up softly and began following her.

She got on the same bus but hid in the crowd. When Pushpa disembarked at Byculla, she too got off and followed her. Pushpa entered a building named Samyukta. Sudha followed her and asked the watchman, 'The person who just went in, which flat did she go to?'

'Who?'

'The girl in the blue salwar kameez.'

'Oh, her! C 42. Every day that girl comes to the same place.'

'Whose house is that?'

'Mehra madam's. Are you interested in a career in films, too?'

'Films?'

'Yes. She is an agent. Agent,' he repeated, winking, 'for everything!'

A large Mercedes-Benz entered the building. The watchman went up and salaamed the person in the driver's seat and helped park the car. 'Go in, ma. If you wish. The first customer is here.'

She felt a chill in the pit of her stomach. She turned and walked away.

The next day, in her usual vivacious manner, Pushpa was making plans for a trip to Dadar Square to eat bhel puri and pani puri when Sudha asked, 'Pushpa, do your relatives live in Samyukta building?' in a most abrupt manner.

Pushpa froze.

'Did you follow me? You spied on me?' she asked angrily.

As the Day Darkens

Sudha's eyes brimmed over. They were both standing under a tree. Pushpa sat on the ground. Seeing Sudha standing, she brusquely ordered her to sit down as well. Once she did that, Pushpa wiped Sudha's eyes and said, 'Why did you come there?'

'Is it all right for you to go there? Do you want to act in the movies?'

Pushpa replied in a very dry voice. 'Sudha, you saw my house, didn't you? What do we have there? Baba who passes his life with idle talk. Aai who is always sick. Two sweet little sisters. All of us have to study. It was when I was in the tenth standard that I met Mehra madam.'

Very softly, Sudha asked, 'Is it prostitution?'

'Something like that. They take nude photos to use on calendars – the face won't be seen, though. But some go further than that. They accompany men to parties. Go to customers' houses. I don't do all those things. And Mehra madam does not force me to.'

When Sudha remained silent, Pushpa said, 'I suppose you will never speak to me again.'

Hugging Pushpa, she said, 'You're always my friend,' and at once Pushpa's face blossomed with a smile.

Pushpa is a famous scientist now. Every year she awards a scholarship to two girls in Ruia College.

One thing led to another and Sudha ended up in the profession that was hers now. She trained under the very highly acclaimed Vidyasagar Rawte. Even now if she wanted some advice she would go to him and him alone, even though he had retired. While scolding his grandchildren for watching detective serials on TV, he continued reading his Agatha Christie, Erle Stanley Gardner, Ed McBain, Dashiell Hammett, Arthur Conan Doyle and Georges Simenon. Even today while pointing out something she had missed, he would say very much in the manner of Sherlock Holmes, 'Elementary, my dear Sudha!'

When Narendra first learnt about her profession, he was indeed shocked. He was a friend who worked in Pushpa's research lab. Pushpa always said that it was a miracle that he had looked past all the lab equipment and the guinea pigs and actually managed to see Sudha.

'So your real business is prying into other people's private lives, is it?'

'I know a lot of your intimate details too.'

'What intimate details?'

'You use Lifebuoy soap. You use Pond's talcum powder. Once a week you apply mustard oil on your body before your bath.'

'What?' he said, his mouth falling open. 'How do you know all that?'

'There is something called a nose, you know.'

'And what else?'

'You like Farida Khanum a lot, especially, "*Aaj jaane ki zid na karo*".'

'How do you know that?'

'You specifically asked for this track at the cassette and CD shop nearby.'

'When?'

'Last week.'

'How do you know that?'

'The shopkeeper keeps a register in which he records the requests of customers. I had gone in on some work and happened to glance at it. You're Dr Narendra Kumar Gupta, aren't you?'

'Wow!'

'I know one more thing.'

'What?'

'You haven't fallen in love before.'

'How do you know *that*?'

'I happened to run into someone who was in college with you. I believe your nickname was "Hermit".'

'O...K...'

'I know one more thing.'

'Tell me. Why leave that one last thing out?'

'You're in love with me.'

'Did you read my diary?'

'No. But last month alone you asked Pushpa about me forty-five times. And that was April. Which only has thirty days. So, forty-five times in thirty days...an average of 1.5 times a day. Don't you think that's a bit excessive?'

He laughed.

'Besides, every time I come close to you I can feel certain chemical changes in you.'

He put his palms together in a gesture of respect and submission. 'I surrender!'

Naren and their eighteen-year-old daughter Aruna had long accepted part of the house being used as her office. Sometimes Aruna would teasingly write on Sudha's notebook requests such as: 'My pink petticoat and orange T-shirt are missing. Please register my case.' Sudha would find the missing items and put them in Aruna's drawer and stick a post-it on the cupboard that said: 'Case successfully solved. My fees: Rs 100.'

Aruna had tuition classes in the evening. She would return only at night. Naren had gone to Delhi for a seminar. When she went towards the kitchen, Chellamma, who had just finished her work, was leaving.

'Chellamma, we'll have a guest later this evening.'

'I've made some extra chapatis. I overheard you talking to Shelke and guessed that someone was coming. Who is she, Sudhamma?'

'A woman and her four-year-old son. Is there any milk?'

'Yes, and also some congee powder. There are some bananas in the fruit basket. Since Aruna does not like bitter gourd, I have made some alu-gobi for her.'

'You really spoil her.'

'She is a child and she is studying hard. If we do not indulge her now, when will we indulge her? She is a child I brought up.'

'I know, you have also raised her taste buds to a high standard.'

'Let it be, Sudhamma!' Chellamma laughed as she picked up her bag and left.

The doorbell rang five minutes after her departure.

∼

It was quite difficult to dig such a big hole. Though they were three, they were panting. So they rested now and then. The sun was slowly sinking. At last it was complete. One of the girls jumped in and the other two pulled her out. 'Hey, elephant calf!' they teased her as they pulled her up. Then she tried to push another of the girls in, then all three of them rushed towards the sea. Every time a wave washed over them, they screamed. The sun's rim touched the horizon.

When Sudha opened the door, Raghav Sawant stood outside with a woman holding a four-year-old by his hand.

Raghav greeted her, told her he would come the next day and took his leave. Sudha asked the hesitant young woman to come in and made her sit at the dining table. She brought her a glass of water.

Sudha began to make some tea. It wasn't really teatime but she felt it would relax the woman if she drank something hot. She warmed some milk, added sugar and two drops of vanilla essence and poured it into a cup with a baby monkey handle and placed it in front of the little boy, saying, 'See, it smells of ice cream!' She took out some biscuits from a tin and put them before him as well. With his eyes on his mother all the while, the child drank the milk and ate the biscuits, dunking them in the milk. The woman sat there looking dazed.

When the kettle light went off, Sudha poured the boiling water over a teabag, added milk and sugar, and placed the cup before the woman.

The woman's eyes brimmed over with tears.

'Didi, my three daughters...'

'Don't worry. Govind is very efficient,' Sudha said to console her.

Once the woman started drinking her tea, Sudha went into her room and opened the cupboard. The woman was very skinny. She would be able to wear a nightdress that was now too small for Sudha. She also took out a salwar kameez set for her for the morning. Her brother's daughter had left behind two sets of her five-year-old son's clothes from a visit a couple of months ago. She took them out for the boy and left everything in Aruna's room. She sent a message to Aruna: 'We have guests at home. You will have to sleep in my room tonight.' Aruna was probably at the bus stop after her tuition class so she replied immediately, 'If that's your command, what else can I do but obey?'

When she got back to the living room, the

woman was sitting on the sofa with her son and staring at the window.

Sudha sat in front of her and said softly, 'You have not told me your name.'

'My name is Archana. This is Dhruv. My husband's name is Gopal.' She sounded exhausted.

'Why don't you freshen up and change your clothes? You look very tired.'

'Didi, my children...' she said again.

'Look here, Govind would surely have started looking for them. You don't have to worry.'

She slowly got up, and Sudha guided her to Aruna's room. When she came out she had washed her face, changed her clothes and changed the little boy's clothes.

When Sudha laid the table and served the two of them hot food, Archana began to cry again.

'He is in the hospital...'

'What can we do at night, Archana? That is a good hospital. They will look after him well. You should eat properly.'

'And you, didi?'

'I'll eat with my daughter when she gets back.'

Slowly she began to eat and at the same time also fed Dhruv. Dhruv's eyes began to shut while he was eating. She wiped his mouth, took him inside and put him on the bed to sleep. She tried to help with the clearing up but Sudha stopped her and took the plates to the sink, wiped the table and brought Archana a glass of water to drink.

'Archana, you should go to bed now. Aren't you tired?'

'Didi, that inspector told me that you're a detective.'

'Yes.'

'Didi, find my daughters for me!' She burst into tears again.

'Archana, this is a police case. It could even be a criminal case. Only the police can sort this out.'

'Let them do what they can. Why don't you make an effort for my sake? I can pay you whatever your normal fees are.'

'Chee chee, it is not about the fee, Archana!'

After a short, silent pause, Sudha said, 'Tell me about your daughters.'

'All three of them are as good as gold. The

As the Day Darkens

eldest, Deepika, is very intelligent. She is in the ninth standard and is the darling of all her teachers. Her favourite teacher is Usha Dikshit, her maths teacher. She cannot stop talking about her. All three girls are my husband's pets. Divya, our second daughter, always follows her father around. Dhwani is just ten, but she has grown so quickly. Didi, he loves his daughters so much...' she said, sobbing.

'Did you wish for a son after the three daughters?'

'No didi, it just happened.'

'You'd come on a weekend trip to the beach resort, hadn't you?'

'Yes didi. Once Deepika moved to the eighth standard, she became rather serious. Too much to study. Also, these days children need private tuitions as well. She is a good student so there are also dance classes, drama classes and all that. That's why I said, let us go somewhere, it'll be good to have a change of scene.'

'The children must have had a good time these two days.'

'A lot of games, fun and food! Only Deepu looked worried now and then. She said she had a lot of work to do, some assignment or something.'

'Her school is co-educational, isn't it?'

'Yes.'

'Is there some boy who is a good friend of hers?'

'Friend? Are you asking about *boy*friends? Didi, she is just fourteen...'

'No, she could have a very good friend, couldn't she?'

'Nothing of that sort.'

'Does she have girlfriends?'

'She is part of a group. Narmada, Shreya, Anupama, Ateesh and Pradeep are part of this group.'

'Oh. Is Divya too in the same school?'

'All three are in the same school. Once Dhruv finishes his UKG, I want to put him there as well.'

'Hm...'

'Wonderful children and a great husband, didi. Someone must have cast an evil eye...'

Archana opened her handbag and showed

Sudha a photograph. It was a photo taken in a studio.

The husband and she. The two of them had their hands on the shoulders of their little boy who stood in front of them. Next to her was the eldest daughter. She was a strong, handsome girl. The two younger girls were in front of the eldest who had her arms around the shoulders of both. The husband's and wife's faces were calm and content. An ideal family.

'A good photograph. Didn't you give it to the police at the station?'

'He too has the same photo with him. We gave that one.'

'Love marriage?'

'Chee chee, arranged by our parents. He was going through a very difficult time then, didi.'

'Why, what had happened?'

'I believe he had a sister called Harshita. She was such a beauty, didi. I've seen her photographs. When he had gone abroad for a few months they found a suitable match for her and fixed her marriage. The wedding invitations were printed.

He too was very happy. But a week before the wedding, Harshita ran away from home...'

'With whom?'

'Who knows? She never came back.'

'Perhaps she did not like the groom?'

'Couldn't she have told them earlier? She was an educated girl. My mother-in-law told me that the groom was in a very good position, working with a shipping company in Singapore. I believe my husband was absolutely shattered by all this. He was very fond of his little sister. But they did not know who she was having an affair with. She had completely concealed it from them.'

'Couldn't they find her?'

'They looked for her everywhere, didi, but they never found her. I never mention the subject to him. You should have heard the way he screamed "I have lost my little girls" today.'

'Poor man.'

'He won't be able to withstand this, didi!' She began to cry again. 'They left saying that they'd go to Aksa beach today because we'll be leaving early in the morning in two days.'

'You did not go?'

'Dhruv had got into the swimming pool. So I did not go. When they were at the beach my husband wandered away for a little while. When he got back they were not there. How could they vanish like that, didi? Somebody must have abducted them – in this city anything can happen! There aren't many people at Aksa beach usually. It's a very beautiful beach. I've been there. He took them there because the children had never seen it. He came back in the same autorickshaw in which they went, howling and beating his chest...'

She began to hit herself on the chest.

Sudha held her hand.

Poor man, so many losses in his life!

Just then the doorbell rang. It was Aruna. When Sudha introduced Archana to her, she said 'Hello' in the midst of her tears.

Sudha took Archana to Aruna's room and then sat down with Aruna to eat her dinner.

When the waves began to rush in with great force, the eldest among them said to her two younger siblings, 'Enough, let's go!' But they kept saying, 'One minute, just one minute!' They even went a bit further and faced the waves. The youngest said, 'Dhinka chika, dhinka chika!' to the waves. A really large wave rose and rushed in. She felt as if someone was pulling her up by the collar of her dress. She quickly drew her younger sisters close. The monster wave which rose like a snake rearing its head slapped them and receded.

When Sudha saw Archana's face in the morning it was evident that she had not slept all night. Her eyes were puffed up. She must have been crying. Sudha gave her a cup of tea. 'Didi, I must see him,' she said in a faint voice.

'Yes, we'll go see him, but first drink your tea,' Sudha said. Dhruv was still asleep.

Sudha went to the window and dialled Govind's number.

'Namashkar didi.'

'Sorry, did I wake you up?'

'Been up for a long while. Didi, how is she?'

'Govind, she wants to go to the hospital to see her husband.'

'Did you speak to her last night?'

'OK! Was that what I was *meant* to do?'

'No, didi, not like that! It's just that I thought that a woman would talk more freely to another.'

'Well, has the minister left?'

'Saw him off on a plane last night.'

'Are you finally free to work on this case?'

'Didi, don't put me to shame! We're not that bad. We have made enquiries at the hotel they stayed in and at Aksa beach. The autorickshaw driver who took them from the hotel was on the other end of the beach. It seems he'd dozed off in the rickshaw. He said there was a nariyalwala beside his rickshaw. We interrogated him as well. He said he had seen the girls playing at a great distance. After that he only saw the man running around and howling in panic. Then the two men went along with the father looking for the girls. But did you speak to her?'

She told him about the details she had got from speaking to Archana the night before.

'Does the eldest daughter have a boyfriend?'

'I believe not.'

'Didi, young girls come from villages to Mumbai hoping to get into Bollywood. Why would these girls want to go away from Mumbai?'

'Were there any bodies washed up?'

'No bodies, didi. By the time we got there, darkness had already set in. The nariyalwala was still there because he had customers from the neighbourhood, but he too was about to leave. We used torches to search the area, but there was nothing. Now, in the morning, we're looking in all those places where we usually find bodies washed up. We have searched the railway stations. I have even sent two people to the village they are from.'

'Not bad, Govind, you've taken prompt action.'

'We're not that bad, didi.'

'Well, if a girl is raped, I know that you'll say the girl has no "character" and give the rapist a good dinner before sending him home!'

'Didi, this is too much!'

'Is there anything wrong in what I said?'

'Didi, that won't happen in my police station.

Don't you know my wife is a human rights activist?'

'Yes, that is a point in your favour, Govind.'

'Go on, didi!'

'Can she go to the hospital now?'

'Yes, and then to her own house.'

'Can you send someone to accompany her?'

'Can you go with her, didi?'

'I could.'

'Didi, then could you do me a small favour? Could you check if there is any diary, letter or anything else in the eldest daughter's room? We can't go in and check for anything without a search warrant. CRPC 1973 rules. We'll get that as well, but I'm working on many things to do with this case now. I'll tell you about it later. I'm really busy now. If we find just one strand, it would be enough. Anyway, if you could search a little in their house...'

She looked at Archana's face when the conversation ended. Archana was just staring into her teacup.

'Archana, don't you want to go to the hospital?'

Startled, Archana looked up. She hurriedly drank her tea.

'I'll have a bath, didi.'

She had washed and hung up her undergarments the previous night. They were dry. Sudha took them off the steel drying stand and gave them to Archana along with a towel and the salwar kameez she had set aside for her the day before.

'No, why didi, I do have the clothes I wore.'

'Never mind, we'll fold them and put them by. You can return these whenever. I am in no hurry to get them back.'

Archana went in to bathe.

Aruna came out of her room ready for college. 'Good morning Ammu!' she said and put the bread slices into the toaster and quickly began making sandwiches. She had morning classes.

Just as Sudha went to get ready, Dhruv woke up and called out for his mother. Aruna spoke sweetly to him and cajoled him to brush his teeth. She had got him dressed by the time Sudha came out.

'Aruna, sit down to eat. You will miss your classes otherwise,' Sudha said and Aruna sat down for her breakfast. Archana came out wearing the clothes given to her – they suited her well. She sat down rather shyly by Dhruv's side. She smiled at Aruna as she helped Dhruv with his food.

Dhruv, who had been silent till then, began to fuss. He pushed away his plate and refused to drink his milk. He screamed and leaped up.

'Ayya, sorry didi! What is wrong with this child?'

'Nothing, he is just frightened. He doesn't understand anything. And he is not able to express that.' Sudha went to Dhruv, who was screaming, kicking his legs and flailing his arms, and said in soothing tones, 'Dhruv, shall you and I look for your three missing sisters? Will you help me?'

Sobbing, he said, 'Didi is not there.'

'Dhruv is a big boy, isn't he, he'll go with the police and find his didi.'

'Deepika didi was crying,' he said.

'When?' Sudha asked.

'That day.'

'Now drink your milk. Look, over there! There is a squirrel on the tree!' she said to divert his attention.

With her bag slung on her shoulder, Aruna

gave them the thumbs-up and said 'All the best!' and left.

After breakfast they set out for the hospital. They went down and Sudha opened the back door of her red Maruti car for them. She took the wheel and started the car. Dhruv remained quiet, staring at the little toy bear that was dangling from the rear-view mirror.

~

Though the car was passing through hilly terrain it was being driven really fast. The wind whooshed and swirled and beat against them. They were silent. He was angry. She looked at his face with some trepidation. 'You wanted to betray me, didn't you?' he asked harshly. 'What could I do?' she stuttered. She was afraid. He had beaten her up before. He was a man of malicious rages. In his hands lay her wings, clipped a long time ago. Nobody at home knew about it. She did not have the courage to tell them. Even on that day she had come out of the house without telling

As the Day Darkens

anyone. Just when she had tried to escape through a small gap in the cage she was locked in, she had been netted again. With the steering wheel in one hand he punched her on the cheek. 'You're mine. You know that, don't you?' he said and yanked her plaited hair hard. 'All of you thought you could hide it from me, didn't you? Will I let you go? And what a handsome bridegroom – bald-headed!' With those words, he rapped her head with his knuckles. She kept staring into the distance. The sun was being swallowed by the crocodile mouth of two hills. Dusk. Faint light mingled with the darkness. Then the darkness swiftly engulfed the evening. The car slowed down along the hillside during a wide U-turn. Just for a second. She opened the door of the vehicle and leaped into the valley below.

There was the usual crowd in the hospital. Rows of chairs. Crying children. Tired eyes. Wilted faces. Archana's husband had just woken up. As soon as he saw his wife and child, he screamed out loud. 'I want to leave,' he screamed like one possessed and tried to run out. Four or five nurses and a ward boy came and restrained him.

'Poor man,' said a nurse and gave him an injection in the arm. In a few minutes he calmed down completely.

Archana stood there crying. The little boy stuck to his mother.

Sudha moved away and called Govind.

'Govind, her husband is still not all right. Shall I take her to her place?'

'Do take her home, didi, please. The cops from Malwani station are cooperating with us and we're investigating this together. Please remember what I told you this morning.'

'OK Govind, I'll try. Can we leave her alone at home? She is very agitated.'

'No didi. I'll send a lady constable there. We won't leave her alone. So many cases of suicide these days.'

'Yes, that's what I meant.' She disconnected the phone.

Archana's husband, though relatively calm, was again trying to escape and was heaving and straining at the restraints.

It was a truly pitiable sight. A weekend holiday

trip had ended with the total devastation of the family!

She consoled Archana and Dhruv. The doctor came in and said that Gopal would have to stay in the hospital for at least another day or two. He had suffered a dreadful shock. Sudha explained the situation to the doctor and left with Archana and Dhruv after informing the constable posted there by Govind.

All the way home Archana's eyes kept welling up with tears but no sound escaped her. It must have been because she didn't want to frighten her son. The little boy was completely subdued.

As soon as they reached their house, Archana sat on the sofa, looking utterly defeated. The little boy sat staring at her. When Sudha fetched a glass of water for Archana, she drank it and continued to sit with a vacant look on her face.

'Archana, have courage,' Sudha said and patted her on the shoulder. 'You told me to also make an effort to find them. May I look around the house a little? Do you have any objection to that?' she asked her softly.

'No didi,' Archana said. She went in to splash some water on her face and came back to guide Sudha around the house.

In the bedroom there was an enlarged version of the small photograph of the three girls she had shown her earlier. Behind the cupboard, and partly obscured by it, was the photograph of a young girl.

'That is Harshita,' said Archana.

Sudha looked at the picture. Harshita wore no make-up in it. She had a sharp nose, large eyes and a slight smile. This was a photograph taken in a studio and she had posed for it with one hand on a three-legged stool. She had brought her plait to the front and it reached well below her waist.

'Archana, may I have this? I'll give it back.'

'Why this, didi? What is the use of this now?'

'Just like that. I'll definitely give this back to you.'

'All right, didi. But be very careful with it. Otherwise he'll be very upset.'

In the shelves on the other side of the room, there were many books. Many Hindi, some English.

As the Day Darkens

'Do you like literature?'

'No, they are all his. I read a few Hindi books. Whenever he travels, he buys a book to read at the airport.'

On the table was a laptop and some files. Nothing had been disturbed. Fortunately, the police had not yet searched the place. Otherwise they would have behaved like an army of monkeys and messed up everything.

Sudha looked through the files on the table. They were all good quality plastic files – letters in connection with his work, some slips of paper, receipts, electricity bill receipts. In some files there were copies of letters that had come in connection with his work. She skimmed through an old-fashioned file that had faded in colour. Letters from his parents, news of relatives, and a wedding invitation. A light yellow card with kumkum-red lettering. There was a tiny illustration of a bride and groom exchanging garlands. It was an invitation to Harshita's wedding. A memento to remember a wedding that never took place. The paper used was thick, glossy and smooth, and it had a transparent tissue overlay. She slowly took it out of the file.

'Why this, didi? A story that happened fifteen years ago. For some reason he has kept it.'

'Don't worry, Archana. Sometimes these little bits of information may help. I told you I'll return these to you. Don't be anxious. In fact, if I could use your computer, I can scan them and return them right now.'

'We have a scanner and printer.' When Archana said this, Sudha slowly opened the back of the photo frame and took out the photograph. Meanwhile Archana turned on the laptop. Sudha scanned the photograph and the invitation and sent them to her email address. She also made hard copies on the printer. The photograph went back into the frame and then to its obscure corner. Archana carefully placed the invitation back in the file.

When she opened the small cupboard in Archana and Gopal's bathroom, she found the usual assortment of shampoo, soap, talcum powder, creams, shaving paraphernalia, amla hair oil and toothpaste on the top shelf. In the lower shelf there was Crocin, Aspro, Amrutanjan, Tiger Balm, Pudin Hara and other such medicines. When she was about to shut the door of the cupboard her eyes lit upon a bottle of Donormyl.

Turning around she asked, 'Archana, who are the sleeping pills for?'

'For him. He's been unable to sleep well for the past two years. It's due to work tension. You know how many different things have to be considered when running a business. He was under a lot of stress. Looking at him I'd get tense.'

The doorbell rang.

It was a woman standing with a bag slung on her shoulder.

Greeting her with 'Come in, teacher', Archana began weeping again. The teacher came in and sat on one of the sofas. Dhruv had gone to sleep on the other.

'I saw it this morning in the paper. Though it was just a small report, I was alarmed when I noticed the names Deepika, Divya and Dhwani. What happened, Archana behen?' the teacher asked.

'Someone has abducted them,' said Archana in the midst of tears.

'Deepika is such a smart and resourceful child,' said the teacher.

'Did she say anything to you recently?' asked Sudha.

'No, Deepika is a girl of few words.'

Sudha left them and walked into another bedroom. It was obvious that this was the children's room. Along one wall was a large cupboard and a long table with four chairs. Next to it was another table with a desktop computer. She opened its drawers. There were pencils, pens, erasers, pins, paper clips and drawing pins scattered all around them. Only one drawer was arranged in an orderly manner. Must be Deepika's, she thought.

She came out and took Archana's leave.

Archana's eyes filled up again. 'Didi, please, you must help, too,' she said.

The teacher requested a ride and asked if she could be dropped off on the way back.

Once they were in the car, the teacher said softly, 'The police have questioned many students who study in Deepika's school. They've also spoken to students from Divya's and Dhwani's classes.'

Sudha thought that that must be one of the 'many things to do with this case' Govind had mentioned.

'My, they've got down to it so quickly!'

'There was huge confusion in the school on seeing the police even though they were in mufti, probably because they didn't want to alarm the kids. The principal was still quite shaken. I did not mention all this to Archana behen. Poor thing, she'd be really frightened.'

'Teacher, Divya and Dhwani are still very small. But may I have the names and numbers of the kids in Deepika's group?'

'But the police have spoken to them already.'

'Well, I just asked.'

'They are all in my class. I do have their numbers.'

'Could you give them to me?'

The teacher opened her bag, took out a sheet of plain paper, wrote down the numbers and gave it to Sudha.

'Such good girls!' she lamented. 'And Deepika is really exceptional. She is not like other girls of her age. She is always very calm. In last week's composition class she had written a beautiful essay.'

'What was it about?'

'About her dreams for the future. Everyone else had written about their future as doctors, air hostesses, business magnates and so on. But Deepika wrote "I would like to be a bird and fly up very high in the sky."'

'It is not uncommon for girls of that age to write poetic stuff like that, isn't that so?'

'Only Deepika did it in my class.'

After dropping off the teacher at a street corner, Sudha parked the car to the side and started dialling the numbers the teacher had given her. When she introduced herself, they were a bit hesitant at first but then opened up, all begging her to find their beloved friend. She also learned that Ashish was her closest friend.

Ashish spoke with a maturity that was far beyond his fourteen or fifteen years. When she

As the Day Darkens

said, 'I hear that you're her best friend,' he replied immediately with caution, 'We're just friends.'

'Just friends?'

'Yes aunty.'

'OK, do you talk to each other a lot on your cellphones?'

'No aunty, we only text each other. Almost all of us do that. In fact, yesterday I sent Deepu two messages.'

'Facebook, Twitter, Orkut...'

'The entire group is on Facebook, aunty.'

'Did Deepika's parents not object?'

'No aunty. Her parents are very nice people.'

'Do you visit her often?'

'We only go when there's a birthday or something. Otherwise all of us in the group meet only at a park or the beach.'

'What is Deepika's ID on Facebook?'

'Deep. D, double E, P, aunty.'

'Does Deepika have an email account?'

'She does, aunty. D, double E, P @gmail.com. We hardly ever use our Gmail accounts. Everything goes through our mobiles or Facebook.'

'Ashish, thanks for helping us find your friend.'

'Aunty, I can help you look into Deepu's Facebook account. Otherwise you'll have to waste a lot of time trying to hack into it. Give me your address, I'll come to your place,' he said at once.

'You're very bright, Ashish!'

'Deepu is my friend, aunty.'

'Don't you have school today?'

'We do, but the police uncle told the principal to let us off today.'

'Oh, do you have to go to the station now?'

'Aunty, we will go wherever you want.'

'Achcha, so shall I call you in ten minutes?'

'OK aunty.'

She called Govind from her cellphone. 'It sounds like you're on the fast track with this!'

'Why?'

'You have asked Deepika's friends to meet you at the station.'

'Didi, we're policemen. We deal with criminal cases, not with ordinary ones like you do.'

'Oh, like the ones where people die of gunshot

wounds or stab wounds with no one actually killing them?'

'Didi, enough of pulling my leg! Is there any news?'

'Deepika must have had a cellphone with her. Where is it? Do you happen to have it by any chance? Where did you find it?'

'Yesterday we kept trying the number. It did not get connected. This morning the phone rang. At first no one answered. But then later in the morning someone did answer the phone. It was the nariyalwala. He says he found it behind a rock where he throws his garbage. He came and gave it to us. He was rather frightened. After that when we went to search the area, we found the bucket and spade. We went to the school to talk to her friends only after we got the phone.'

'Was there any...'

'No didi. There were only missed calls from last night. The calls we made from the station, the calls that the parents made, and two messages – jokes sent by Ashish.'

'Did you check the time when the messages were sent?'

'Didi, do you think we're nincompoops? The messages had come at nine and just after. Perhaps because he didn't know how to erase them, he just left them in the inbox. All that is well and good, didi, but am I investigating this case or are you? You're piling one question on top of another!'

'Hey Govind! It's just that I am a bit worried after speaking to Archana. You seem to have taken it amiss.'

'Didi, can't you take a joke? I just said that in jest. Then? Next question?'

'It looks like the man who kidnapped the children was in a hurry. Don't you think so, Govind? He seems to have thought about the cellphone only after he hid the plastic bucket and spade behind the rocks. So it looks like he flung it there without even turning it off. Perhaps he thought it would get damaged by the force with which it was flung. Fortunately it fell on sand and did not break. Am I right?'

'Absolutely, didi! It was the nariyalwala who

switched off the phone. What other news, didi?'

'Govind, when they were being abducted, do you think three smart girls would have done nothing at all?'

'He could have had a weapon, didi. They would have been frightened by it. Besides, it turns out the nariyalwala had gone away to relieve himself. The "toilet" is only a wall but it's at a distance. Those ten minutes are important. He could have taken advantage of that window. The autorickshaw driver was asleep all through. Perhaps that is why nobody knows anything. Didi, later we will question the auto driver and the nariyalwala further. I don't intend to take their word as the absolute truth. This is only the beginning. And was there a laptop or desktop computer in their house, didi?'

'There are two, Govind.'

'Once we get a search warrant we will go there this very afternoon. How is Archana ma'am doing?'

'She's very worried, of course. How is her husband?'

'The doctors say he still needs a few more days of rest in the hospital.'

'OK.'

'Then, didi?'

'When the school group leaves the police station, can you send them to me, please? I'd like to make an attempt to talk to them as well, just to see what information I can get.'

'Were you able to find anything in their house, didi? I don't know what we'll get from our search. We are sure to get some fingerprints but I don't really know if that'll be of any use.'

'Just make sure your people handle it without upsetting Archana.'

'I'll send only those who've had special training under me. I might even go myself because Archana ma'am looked very distressed last evening.'

'You've got all your good un-policeman-like qualities from your wife, Govind!'

'You cannot let a day pass without taking a dig at me, can you, didi? But go on.'

'I brought the sister's photo and wedding invitation. I told you about that before.'

'That is of no use at all, didi. What is the connection between that case and this?'

'I know that. But you know how my guru would say even a small twig can help.'

'Oh, those dated, old-fashioned tactics! It has all changed now, didi. Right, I'll send the school group to you.'

She called Ashish and informed him about that.

~

Deepika's Facebook profile picture was fuzzy at first. Then it transformed into a bird. Then it became the sky, then the sea, a flower dripping honey and then a little girl hidden behind an umbrella, and then a faceless body. Views of an extended arm, a single ear, closed eyes and plaited hair followed.

In her photos with her friends, she always seemed to keep herself at a slight distance from the others. Her face was always lowered. She often hid behind the rather fat Ashish and only a part of her face could be seen. In the photographs with her sisters, they always stood on either side of her and she had her arms firmly on their shoulders. At the school farewell function she was wearing a parrot green sari tinged with pink. There was a photo where the sari's pallu was flying in the wind and her head was flung backward with her face turned to the sky, her fair neck glowing in the light – she looked like a green parrot poised to fly.

Vidyasagar Rawte listened very patiently to all that Sudha had to say. Then he asked her what sort of things Deepika had written on her Facebook page.

'The usual things, guruji. The stuff that kids that age write about. Nothing different. She seems rather shy.'

'Hm...'

He began to narrate a number of Facebook-related stories: an American woman who, through Facebook, found her biological mother who had abandoned her in an orphanage; family members separated during Partition who had found one another through Facebook; a man believed to have died in a concentration camp during the Second World War found by his sister's daughter through

Facebook; long-lost lovers reunited on Facebook. And wasn't it on Facebook that an artist who had remained a spinster found her life partner at the age of sixty? Rawte also told her that he too had a Facebook account but had not managed to trace his old flames. There was no chance of his finding a new lover either. People thought of him as a grandfatherly old man, he laughed.

He was indeed getting old, she thought.

A short while later when she got up to leave, just as she reached the door, he said, 'That poor man! Whoever he loves disappears suddenly.'

Startled, she looked at him.

He winked.

∼

The houses in the foothills were very old. Houses in which many generations of families had lived. Prabhusagar Nigam had founded a very large school in that town. He could have lived in one of the town's upscale areas. But he did not want to leave his ancestral home. New families had moved into the adjacent houses. The younger generation of his family lay scattered in various countries of the world. His wife, who had gone to Canada for their daughter's childbirth, had mingled with the ocean on her way home in the Kanishka air crash of 1985. She had been mortally afraid of water. Her face would in fact turn pale during the rains. And she had dissolved into the waters in the end. The letter that she had last written to him before she left Canada reached him later. While describing how gorgeous their granddaughter was, it also gently expressed her love for him, saying she had begun to miss him badly.

He had been extremely lonely since then. He took to rambling in the hills for long hours. He began to buy diaries every year and keep a record of all that he had done during the day. When he read those entries, he liked what he found there and wondered if he should have chosen to be a writer. His entry for 22 August 1995 was:

Today was a very different kind of day.
As usual I went for a walk in the evening. From

As the Day Darkens

a thick wild bush on the slope of the hill I heard groans and whimpers. I thought a cow or a goat must have strayed and stumbled and fallen into it while grazing. When I listened more carefully I realized that the sounds were human. I used my torch to try and look into the bush. The foliage was so thick and wild that I could see nothing. With difficulty I climbed up and then with my cane I parted the branches and began to search. There was a girl inside the bush, one of her legs bent at an unnatural angle. When she saw me, she said, in a feeble voice, 'Please, help me!' I slowly helped her up and tried to make her stand. The leg that was bent was swollen. She groaned in pain. She kept looking around, obviously scared of something. She put her palms together in entreaty and looked at me, saying nothing. Her cheeks were wet from the copious tears she had shed. I gave her my walking stick and, making her walk slowly, brought her home. I gave her some hot milk and some painkillers. She appeared very tired and closed her eyes soon after.

After about half an hour, I heard a car come to a stop outside. Normally only scooters and motorbikes ply these roads. It was rare to encounter a car. I went to the window and saw a black car standing at a distance. In the faint light from the street lamps I saw a young man get out of it. He focused the car headlights on various bushes on the hills, seemingly looking for something. When the doors of some of the houses around opened, he asked them something. Around ten men went out with torches to look into the bushes.

The young man then walked towards me and stood by the window to ask, 'Saheb, did you see something here about two hours ago?'

'Something? What do you mean?'

'A girl. Did she...'

'Girl? Only cows or goats fall into bushes in these parts. No human beings have ever fallen in so far.' Before I could ask him anything, he had turned stiffly on his heel and walked off towards the car.

When I turned, the girl was standing by the sofa, cane in hand, her face bleached of colour.

Outside, there was the sound of the car moving away.

As the Day Darkens

I reassured her and guided her back in. I knew that it was the time of day when Dr Haridas returned home from the hospital. Since his house was on the street right next to mine, I thought that rather than explain everything on the phone, I would go and talk to him in person and bring him over. I told her to get some rest and stepped out.

Hari was late this evening. I explained everything to him and brought him home. Thinking she would find it difficult to come and open the door, I did not ring the bell. I opened the door with my key and went to the inner room, but she was not there! I searched the kitchen and the other rooms. She had vanished! The back door had been unlocked and just pulled shut. My cane had also disappeared! It was Hari who showed me the note on the table. It said 'Thank you very much' and was written on the back of a receipt left on the table. My black pen had been placed on it.

For a long while she kept looking at Harshita's photograph. Then she looked at the invitation card.

'Stella, call Pooja please!'

Stella dialled the number and gave her the phone.

'Pooja, it's Sudha.'

'Tell me, are you coming to Jaipur?'

'No, I've a small request. I need some help.'

'I hope it won't be something that will land me in trouble!'

'Nothing like that. I just want the telephone number of someone called K.C. Shrivatsav.'

'There are many Shrivatsavs in Jaipur. Do you know the full name – what K.C. stands for?'

'No, but I do have his address.'

'Oh, that'll help. When do you need it?'

'Right now.'

She put the phone down and in exactly fifteen minutes Pooja called and gave her the information.

Stella called the number and after ascertaining that it was indeed K.C. Shrivatsav, she gave the phone to Sudha, whispering, 'Sounds like a very old man.'

'Namashkar Shrivatsavji.'

As the Day Darkens

'Namashkar. But I'm afraid I do not know who you are.'

'My name is Sudha Gupta. My husband and your son worked together in Singapore a long time ago.'

'Yes, go on.'

'It has been a long time. They did not keep in touch. Where is your son now?'

'Still there, in the same company.'

'How is he? We heard that his marriage got cancelled at the last minute.'

'Yes, that was a most unfortunate incident. It was so humiliating. The girl ran away.'

'With whom?'

'Who knows?'

'I'd like your son's telephone number.'

'I only know his mobile number. He has told me that I should never give it to anybody without his permission.'

'That's OK. He must have been very badly affected by this incident.'

'But it's been fifteen years since it happened!

Anyway, he was never very open about his feelings. I don't know if it was because of the way that whole thing happened, but within three months of it he got married to a girl in a registrar's office and came here with her. Told me it was love.'

'So you did get a daughter-in-law in the end!'

'The girl he had been engaged to was said to be a real beauty. But I had cataracts in my eyes and could see her only as a shadow. This girl was also quite good-looking. But I know nothing about this love business. I'm now eighty-five years old. I never talk about all that. I used to go to Singapore regularly once a year till about five years ago. Now I cannot do that. We only talk on the phone. He has no time even to breathe. They never come here. She too works in some school. Anyway, what with the children's education and so on...'

'Sorry to have bothered you so much, sir. Forgive me.'

'No beti. That's all right. Namashkar.'

He rang off.

The name of the company the groom worked in was mentioned in the wedding invitation. She did not know where she was going with this bit of the investigation. She bent her head, thought for a few moments and then gave Stella the company's name and asked her to Google it. Within five minutes she got the address, telephone numbers, map – everything. She called the number given there. A synthetic metallic voice announced the name of the company and then went on to give her numerous choices – press this for that or another for something else – and at last when she had lost hope that she would ever be able to get a human voice at the other end, there was one.

'May I help you?'

'I'd like to speak with an engineer in your company, Mr Sharad Shrivatsav. I'm calling from India.'

'Please wait,' the voice said and she could hear her trying to connect the call. Tchaikovsky played on the line.

Then a voice came through.

'Hello, it's Sharad Shrivatsav. How may I help you? I was told you are calling from India.'

It was not a harsh voice. It sounded friendly.

'I'm sorry to disturb you. I'm a private detective. My name is Sudha Gupta.'

'What?' shouted the voice at the other end. 'Why are you calling me?' His tone made it clear that he was distancing himself. She was afraid he might even cut the call.

'Don't be upset, Mr Shrivatsav. I'm just hoping you might somehow help with a case I'm investigating. It may not help at all. Please, can we talk for about ten minutes?'

'What case, Sudhaji? Look here, I have no time to get involved in anything like this, nor do I have any wish to.'

'Just five minutes, Mr Shrivatsav! Please...'

'Well, OK, ask. Are you recording this?'

'No, no. Don't worry.'

She told him about what had happened during the last two days. She explained to him that she had begun to look into a fifteen-year-old incident because she had found no clues to the sudden disappearance of the children and hoped that she might find some thread she could grasp at by pursuing this line of enquiry. She told him that she had spoken to his father. He listened to her without interrupting her. Finally, she asked him about his marriage being called off.

'Yes. That marriage got stalled. I have no connection with that family,' he said.

Sudha was silent.

'But I did get married,' he said softly.

'Your father told me. To someone you fell in love with, right?'

'Yes. Her name is Harshita.'

This time the loud cry came from her side.

~

He felt it wasn't a big deal. That was why Ashish had not said anything about it. Anupama would send at least twenty jokes or funny news items. Shreya would call even at one o'clock at night and giggle as she talked. Narmada was his very close friend. He was in love with her. She too was in love with him. But the two families did not know about this. Everyone in the group did. Deepika would act as if she was older than everyone else. She would hang around with everyone, listen to them, laugh, talk, play. But in some way she would hold herself apart. She'd never get really close to anyone. They were all her friends. But sometimes she would act very odd. When they had all gone on a school trip, everyone got into the swimming pool and fooled around. She did too. Though they had been warned a few times not to go to the deep end, she began to swim towards it. It was he who shouted out and warned her. It did not seem to be by accident that she behaved so. It seemed like a deliberate attempt. When he confronted her about it she would not give him a response.

'Are you shocked?' asked Sharad Shrivatsav.

'Yes.'

'It's a long story.'

'Will Harshita talk to me?'

'How will talking to Harshita help?'

'Actually, I don't know how that'll help.'

'Anyway, let her decide. Do you have a Skype account?'

'I do.'

He gave her Harshita's Skype identity. He told her that she should call her at 10 p.m.

'Thank you very much. I'll talk to Harshita tonight. I'm sorry to have bothered you.'

'Not at all. If this will help in some way to locate the three children, this is no bother at all. Besides, I get the feeling that you're not the wrong kind of person. All the best.'

Stella was still there, looking at her expectantly. It was time for Stella to leave.

Sudha was rather confused. Was she going in a totally wrong direction? Besides, the case wasn't even hers. It had been taken up by Govind and his team. But the memory of Archana pleading with her to take up the case kept haunting her. Let tonight's effort be the last, she thought. Then she would leave it to Govind and his people.

Chellamma had arrived. Stella got up and fetched the cinnamon tea.

'Sudhamma, shall I stay the night?'

'Why, Stella?'

'To connect you on Skype.'

'Aruna can do it.'

'Let me also stay, Sudhamma.'

'Hey, can't you wait to find out in the morning?'

'I could but I'm very eager to know. And Gupta sir is out of town in any case. Will it be such an imposition if I stay?'

Chellamma had the ears of a snake. She began to make Stella's favourite dish: capsicum stuffed with a filling of mashed potatoes flavoured with garam masala.

When the Skype call was made at ten o'clock that night, Harshita's face appeared on the screen.

―

Though she had tried twice, it had been to no avail. Ashish had prevented it. She had no desire to live. She had intended to get buried in the depths of the swimming pool. 'Life is extremely cruel. It is like a worm that snakes through the body. I want to die…' When she was writing this on the last page of her school exercise book, she heard her mother screaming. Startled, she turned and her mother shook her, saying, 'What is this? What is this?' Hearing her mother say this, she broke down. She told her mother. Her mother glared at her and tore the page out. 'You know how much your father will suffer if he hears such things. Sit down and study.' She placed her hand on her shoulder and angrily forced her to sit and then left the room. Dhruv came in and stood watching her cry.

~

Harshita looked just as pretty as she did in her photo. She greeted Sudha and said, 'I believe you wish to speak to me.'

'Yes. My name is Sudha Gupta. This is my assistant, Stella.'

'Hello.'

'Pardon us for bothering you. We're disturbing you even though we're not sure if there's even any connection with the case in my hands.'

'That's all right. What did you want to speak about? I'll speak on the condition that you will not use my name or what I say in a direct manner. I only agreed to speak because of the children.'

'We won't use anything without your permission, even if it helps in some significant way. If I tell the concerned people and they approach you, you will cooperate, won't you? For the sake of three lovely girls, you will do it, won't you?'

'It was for them that I agreed to this. Go ahead.'

'What happened before the cancellation of your wedding plans? Why did you disappear without saying anything?'

'I was being abused. There was this man harassing me constantly. I was in his clutches. I was a real coward then, too scared to tell anyone. He did not like the fact that I was getting married. He insisted that I should say I don't want to get married and stop it from happening. He took me in his car on a hillside road and threatened me. At a point where the road turned, I jumped into the valley below. I could not think of anything in my state of panic...'

She stopped for a while and closed her eyes.

'An old man saved me. One of my legs got twisted when I fell and it swelled up badly. The old man took me to his house and saved me from my abuser when he came looking for me. But when the old man went to fetch a doctor, I called Sharad from the phone in his house. He came and took me away. We left by the back door. Poor old man, I even took away his walking stick as I needed it. I still keep it in memory of the kind gentleman. I stayed in Jaipur at the home of one of Sharad's friends and had to have three months of treatment. Everything was done in a secret manner.'

'But how come you spoke to Sharad...'

'The day he came for the bride-viewing ceremony, I told him everything. He knew it all.'

'But why did you have to call Sharad?'

'Even if I went back home, I couldn't tell them about this. I'd have had to say that I didn't want this marriage and that the wedding arrangements should be stopped. They could not have borne it. If I got completely lost, it would remain a mystery forever.'

'You were that scared of that man? What did he do that you were so afraid of him?'

Harshita did not answer at once. Then she said softly, 'That man had been abusing me since I was twelve years old. He also kept threatening me.'

'Abuse as in...'

'Sexually...'

After a short silence Sudha asked, 'A man bothers you, abuses you sexually. But Sharad was an outsider, could you not have told your brother what you eventually told Sharad? He was someone who loved you dearly. I hear that your parents were broken-hearted. Frightened of some man, you gave them such pain. Sorry! I've said too much, haven't I?'

'No ma'am. There's nothing wrong in what you said. I couldn't tell anybody about that man. I felt they would not be able to comprehend it. Mine was a family that believed in family honour and principles. I could not come to terms with it myself. The only reason I became a whole human being again was because of Sharad.'

'Couldn't you even tell your beloved brother? He would have helped, surely! I was told he went crazy after that.'

'He definitely could not have helped. Because the man who abused me from age twelve was my brother.'

Sudha was stunned. Harshita looked at her, her eyes were brimming with tears.

'If the Ganga is soiled, where can one go to wash away one's sins?' she said in Hindi, sobbing.

~

Of all the states in the country, the number of convictions in criminal cases is the lowest in Maharashtra because the investigative teams rarely ever collect evidence using forensic science. Except in the cases that attract public attention, the police never bother to do so. Even though there is a police academy in Pune, the police here do not show any interest in gathering forensic evidence. They only spend their time interrogating witnesses.

Times of India

Govind Shelke was an exception. He took great interest in the examination of forensic evidence gathered from blood samples, hair follicles, fingerprints, cigarette butts, footprints, voiceprints and such, and worked with Dr Swarupa Hegde, who used software programs and lab work in the analysis of evidence. He was an ace at using metallic dusting powders, liquids, vapours and such commonly used substances to collect fingerprints. He then recorded them on a digital camera and lifted them on to clear adhesive tape without missing any of the loops, whorls or arches on them. They had both participated in the special training course recently conducted by Scotland Yard. There they learnt to use the newly developed adhesive discs, which looked similar to regular gel tape, to record fingerprints on them. When subjected to certain chemicals the prints glowed in different colours. Depending on the colour one could figure out if the person was a diabetic, a smoker or even a vegetarian. They hadn't yet started using that method though.

Govind made forensic evidence collection a part of all cases, causing irritation and amusement amongst his colleagues in the station. He had sought Dr Hegde's assistance in this case as well.

Ashish was the first person to call her that

morning. He preferred speaking to Sudha as he was a little afraid of the police.

'Aunty, there is something that I did not tell you.'

'What is it?'

He told her about what had happened in the swimming pool.

'Aunty, this was on my mind. Perhaps it's not important. But still, I wanted to tell you about it.'

'Thanks Ashish.'

Just as the call ended the phone rang again, singing, '*Oh re manwa tu toh bawra re...*'

This time it was Archana.

She told Sudha about the police searching the place. Then, 'Didi, one more thing...' She hesitated.

'What is it, Archana?'

'Perhaps it is a very small thing. But...'

'Tell me, Archana.'

'You know how children say idiotic things at times...'

'Who said what, Archana?'

'Deepika...' she said and went on to describe

what her daughter had written in her notebook. About how she had held her by the shoulders and shaken her in anger, and how she had blabbered some nonsense after that.

'What was the nonsense, Archana?'

'Absolute nonsense. She said her father came to her room at night and misbehaved with her.'

'What?!'

'That must have been a dream. For the last two years he has been regularly taking sleeping pills to sleep at night.'

'Wait, wait, Archana...' she said, interrupting her. Droplets of sweat began to form on her face. She calmed herself before speaking again. 'Please repeat that very clearly and slowly.'

'I already told you. Deepika said that her father was behaving badly, coming into her room at night. I think what Deepika said is all nonsense. When they came and searched and asked if she had a diary of some sort, I suddenly remembered this. I felt bad about telling them this and that is why I'm telling you. I don't understand anything, didi. I don't even know if I should talk about what she said or not. Poor man. He was someone who slept with the help of sleeping pills…' There was a sobbing sound.

'Don't cry, Archana.'

'I don't understand anything, didi!'

'OK then, shall we talk later?'

'No, didi, we can talk now.'

'Think carefully and tell me, when did he take the sleeping pills?'

'What kind of question is that, didi! When do people take sleeping pills? Before going to sleep, of course! He would warm up the milk and pour it into two glasses for the two of us. He always worried that I did not look after myself as I should. He would say that between the housework and the children, I had to really struggle to keep up and take care of everything. He would say that I had to drink the Horlicks and Bournvita bought for the children. He was quite right. Only after I started drinking something like that at night, I began to sleep well.'

'Archana…' Sudha said with tenderness, and then told her in a soft voice, 'I think he gave the sleeping pills to you.'

'Why to me?'

'To do what you said Deepika blabbered about.'

'Didi...' she cried, and sobbed.

'Archana, I hope you're not alone at home?'

'No. A neighbour is here with me. A lady constable is also here.'

'Did anybody call you, demanding money?'

'No,' she said as she sobbed and told her that the police had also asked if someone had called asking for money.

'If something like that happens, you must phone Govind first, OK?'

'Didi, about what I said now...'

'I have to tell Govind, I don't know in what way it will help. He has to decide that.'

'Will his reputation be spoilt because of this?'

'What is this, Archana, your daughter has told you this and cried. But you're concerned about your husband's reputation! I don't know, Archana, what to make of mothers like you.'

'No didi, don't get angry with me. She is at an awkward in-between age. It could even be a figment of her wild imagination.'

'Let that be. I'll call you again later.'

She got in touch with Govind and gave him the details of her conversations with Harshita, Ashish and Archana.

'My God, that's really shocking!'

'Govind, my blood is boiling.'

'Didi, I too feel the same way.'

'No Govind. I don't think you take such things seriously.'

Govind disagreed. Then he said, 'I too saw the bottle of sleeping pills. I had it tested for fingerprints, along with the other things around it. They all had Gopal's prints.'

'How do you have his prints?'

'You remember when he came here, he was in a state of panic. At that time we gave them both glasses of water.'

'Oldest trick in the world.'

'Yes didi. Sometimes we too have to use some really old-fashioned tricks. When I ask someone to bring water, my colleagues in the station start rolling their eyes. That day I could hear them mutter under their breaths about my getting the fingerprints of even those who come to lodge a complaint.'

'Well...'

'Didi, another thing. Dr Hegde phoned just now.'

'Tell me.'

'Gopal's fingerprints are on the plastic cover of Deepika's phone as well. And also on the plastic toys.'

'Is it a big deal if his fingerprints are on his daughter's mobile phone?'

'True. But it's possible that he threw his daughter's mobile behind the rocks, isn't it?'

'That's mere speculation. There should be a reason for it, shouldn't there?'

'True. But we could use this to set up a little interrogation drama. Because there are only three sets of fingerprints on it.'

'Govind, the way he behaved with Harshita and Deepika, is that just an irrelevant detail?'

'No didi. We thought the children had been abducted but they've run away in fear.'

'I feel that it could even be suicide, Govind.'

'Will they commit suicide wearing their footwear? Besides, not one body has been found. In order to sever all contact, Deepika herself could have thrown the plastic stuff behind the rocks. And the mobile too for the same reason.'

'But I feel there's something that we're doing wrong here.'

'I need to speak to Archana ma'am and Harshita ma'am. You have to prepare them for that. They might both have misgivings about talking to the police about this. And don't worry, didi. Everything will be clear in tomorrow's interrogation. We will ask solid questions based on the information you've given us today.'

'This is not just information, Govind. It's a criminal act. The case could be turned on its head because of this.'

'Definitely. I'll not let that fellow go free. We could ask Archana ma'am to file a case against him.'

'Govind, shall we ask Harshita to come here? With the shock of seeing her, Gopal might confess to having raped her and Deepika.'

'I thought about that too. Perhaps we should have a video conference.'

'I'll talk to her. You too try speaking to her. She will do this for the children's sake. We'll try to persuade her.'

'Tomorrow at ten, we will bring Gopal straight from the hospital to the station.'

'May I come too, Govind?'

'By the rulebook, you should not be there. But you could accompany Archana. We will bring her here in the morning.'

'Thanks Govind.'

When she got in touch with Harshita and gave her the details, she was shattered. When asked if she could come, she was hesitant. 'I am frightened,' she said. After further conversation, she agreed to speak to Govind. She also said that she would come with her husband.

'There is a Jet Airways flight at five in the afternoon. We'll try to come by that.'

'Should I book a hotel room for you?'

'No. We have friends in Mumbai. Could you

ask the inspector to speak to me? Sharad and I need more information.'

'Definitely, Harshitaji.'

She called Archana and quickly caught her up on all that they knew. She could only hear heavy breathing at the other end. She also told her that Govind would be speaking to her. Sudha then called Govind and gave him the number in Singapore.

Once he had spoken to Sudha, Govind got in touch with DCP Joseph Pinto. All the police officers were rather wary of Pinto as he was a strict disciplinarian. He knew the rules and regulations thoroughly. He also knew many languages. It was a mystery to all as to where he was from, who he was. His wife was Parsi; his children spoke in English. Once, when a man who had been wrongly accused in a kidnapping case was cursing his fate muttering to himself in Tamil, Pinto had asked him, in Tamil, which village in Tirunelveli he was from. Since then, it became generally known that he was a Madrasi. Many were rendered rather uncomfortable given the number of insulting remarks they had made against Madrasis in his presence. Pinto pretended he had not noticed their discomfiture.

Govind gave him the details of the case and said that it would be helpful if he could be present the next day. Whenever he had a friendly conversation with Govind, Pinto spoke in Marathi or Hindi, so when Pinto asked Govind in English what his expectations were for the next day, Govind replied with great caution.

'Sir, a confession?'

'Confession of what, Govind? Please speak clearly.'

'Sir, that it was his behaviour that drove his daughters away...'

'You know that a confession statement will not hold in a court of law. And it could also be just an indirect motive for their disappearance. How will it help in taking the case forward?'

'Sir, the Justice Malimath Committee Report says that a confession made on an audio or video recording can be admitted if a very senior officer is present once we tell the accused that he is allowed to have a lawyer present...'

'You know the kind of criticism that has been levelled at the Malimath Committee Report, don't you?'

'I know, sir.'

'Along with the confession statement, if some major object of evidence such as the murder weapon or the body is found, then it can be taken as proof of the crime. All you have are some fingerprints, some reports of rape. Do you think a confession will give us conclusive proof? What strong piece of evidence do you think you'll be able to find in this instance? You say that maybe the girls ran off on their own. Besides, he is not even an accused here. He was the one who filed the FIR, right? Aren't you being rather hasty? Don't jump the gun!'

'Sir, it's not unusual for the criminal to file the first information report.'

'Other than rape, I don't see any other crime here. Yes, that is a crime. But a separate case has to be filed in that connection. It is very difficult to establish any direct link between that and the disappearance of the kids, Govind.'

'I know, sir. But I do feel that there is some thread here. Sir, if you come...'

'OK, I'll come. Within one hour I want all the relevant information pertaining to this case on my desk. And he should not get mentally affected by the drama you're setting up for him.'

'No sir, a counsellor, Madhu Bhushan, will be there. I'll make all the arrangements very carefully. Within an hour those details will be with you, sir. My preliminary reports will also be emailed to you.'

'I admit, one does feel like beating the hell out of such a monster. But be careful. We have still not proved anything. We have to question the sister and we should speak to the wife.'

'Sir, Sudha Gupta has spoken to the wife and the sister. And I too will speak to them.'

'So Sudha Gupta is on this case as well?'

'Sir...'

'No, no. I have no objection to that. In a way her guru is also my guru.'

'Sherlock Holmes kind of style, sir.'

'We cannot reject that style completely, Govind. And you too once said that you're not in complete agreement with the narco analysis, lie detector and brain mapping tests that were used in the Telgi case and the Nithari murders case.'

'Only when the questioning method fails should it lead to that stage, sir. There are many different ways of handling a case which can all yield very good results, sir. That is why Sudha Gupta...'

'I am not criticizing you at all for asking Sudha Gupta to join in. Don't worry. I know her talents. She is a very capable Madrasi,' he said and laughed.

'Sir...' said Govind hesitantly.

'All right, I too would like to speak to the sister and the wife. Make the necessary arrangements.'

'Sure, sir.'

Then he connected to the number in Singapore.

~

The investigative agency known as the CID is a special branch of every state's police force. Those who work there do not wear uniforms. They work wearing plain clothes which are generally referred to as 'mufti'. The CID has divisions within it such as the state crimes investigation bureau, the fingerprints division and the scientific section. Like their counterparts in the Law and Order police, the CID has its own hierarchy of senior officers and people who work under them. The CID takes up complicated assignments such as those involving communal riots, circulation of counterfeit currency or complex murder cases when the local police along with their normal duties find it tough to allot time or personnel. But the CID can take up a case only when ordered by a judicial court, the Director General of Police, or the government.

Wikipedia

Govind had solved a number of complicated cases successfully. None of the cases he'd taken up were considered badly handled and in need of the CID. He had brought several cases to their conclusion because he used private detectives like Sudha Gupta. Though many were jealous of his success, everyone respected him. Young people who had heard about him and came to see him were generally disappointed. He did not even remotely look like a movie hero playing the part of a policeman. Although he had gone through all the necessary training in defensive tactics there was nothing in the records to say that he had beaten up a criminal or fought furiously with ten ruffians. He did not even have the protruding police belly that was the object of everyone's jokes.

When Govind met Harshita and Sharad the next day, his un-policeman-like personality surprised them. This made it easier for them to talk to him openly.

Harshita and Sharad Shrivatsav were staying with some friends in Amboli. Early in the morning they had rented a taxi and gone to meet Archana. Harshita's heart ached at the thought that she was meeting her sister-in-law for the first time in such terrible circumstances. Archana, who embraced her, bemoaned her own predicament and began to cry. Harshita and Sharad consoled her. Dhruv, who had been sleeping, got up and came out. He looked at the strangers and hesitated but soon sat with full confidence on Sharad's lap. Leaving him in the care of the neighbours, all three left to meet Govind. The way Joseph Pinto spoke to them calmed their nerves. He did not rush anything but explained everything calmly. When Sudha came along with Archana, Pinto greeted her in Tamil: 'Come in, how is your work?'

A little later, Govind talked to them. The conversation was easy and proceeded without any interruptions. When he had told them everything, they sat in a room where they could not be seen by anybody.

At ten when Gopal came in, he was very agitated. He did not look like someone who was a big shot in business circles. He looked worn out. He insisted he had to go home at once. The police had not performed their duties properly, he said, adding that he was very disappointed by this. It had been three nights and two days since the incident. Had the police still not been able to find his daughters? He had no other option but to go to the higher-ups in the police department for help, he said angrily. Govind calmed him down and gave him some tea. He told him in a calm and gentle voice that they were making every effort possible and that the girls would definitely be found very soon. Then he suggested that perhaps Gopal's daughters had run away somewhere. Why would they run away, Gopal countered. Govind told him he wondered if they were frightened of something and so he was looking into that angle. Govind continued with his speculations: that he was filled with great pity for Gopal since it looked like whoever Gopal loved deeply somehow kept disappearing. Didn't you lose your sister too, he pointed out. Gopal jerked his head and turned in Govind's direction and said that there could be no connection between the loss of his daughters and what had happened fifteen years ago. Govind persisted that perhaps there *was* some connection, when, right on cue, Harshita walked into the room. First shock, then anger and then confusion flowed in waves on Govind's face. He tried standing up, holding on to the table, and then gave up. His face turned white as a sheet of paper from which the colours had seeped away. Then Archana too entered the room. When Govind said that his daughters would also be found very soon and that Deepika, Divya and Dhwani would explain why they had run away, a strange howl, like that of a wounded beast, erupted from Gopal.

After that he was totally broken.

His sobs sounded more like hisses. Dr Madhu Bhushan came and patted him consolingly on his back. Govind Shelke told him that he could get his lawyer to come to the station. Sobbing, he gave them the name of his lawyer, and the lawyer came in a while. He advised him repeatedly that he did not have to say anything as no case had been registered against him. But Gopal said that everything had slipped out of his hands and, after folding his hands before Archana and Harshita as if seeking their forgiveness, he went into a frenzy and confessed everything. This was recorded on audio and video. As he spoke, Archana slowly slumped down. Harshita's eyes overflowed with tears. The entire police station froze. When Govind Shelke put handcuffs on him Gopal did not resist.

As the Day Darkens

Excerpts from Gopal's confession:

I used to go to Deepika's room every night. She was the fruit of the seed I had sown and I thought I had the right to taste it. But she resisted me. She fought. She was abusive. I had to use physical force to control her. I gave Archana sleeping pills and indulged in this every night for two years. It was Deepika who made a mistake. She first threatened suicide. Then she said that she would definitely stop me from eyeing her sister and that she would go to the police. She said she would show everyone who I really was. She should not have said that. I got scared.

I made plans for a holiday at a beach resort. At Aksa beach I told them to dig a deep hole and play. A really deep hole. When all three of them were playing in the sea at twilight, I crept up behind them and pushed their heads into the water with these hands of mine. Then I dragged them and pushed them into the hole they had dug. I threw whatever I could find into the hole and filled it up with sand. It did not take me very long. I knew that the area would go underwater during high tide. Only after I closed it up did I see that the cellphone was lying on the corner of a large rock along with the plastic toys. I threw the plastic things behind a large rock in the distance and flung the cellphone hard. I was sure it would be shattered.

During low tide Gopal showed them the spot. They went to the point where the rocks divide the beach into two parts and began digging. As they dug a stench began to fill the air. When they went deeper they found the three girls lying there like three sleeping children – one on her back looking skyward and the other two with their faces buried in the sand. On top of them were some plastic bags and footwear.

It took a long while for the photographer to forget the scene. For the first time in his career, the forensic pathologist choked up when he had to examine the dead bodies.

With Govind's carefully worked-out case, it took less than a year for the court to arrive at a decision. Though Gopal's lawyer tried to argue along the lines of temporary insanity, the court sentenced him for life. Within five years a higher court confirmed the life sentence.

For those five years Archana followed the court proceedings with a wooden face and she never once looked at Gopal. When the life sentence was confirmed, she had no tears in her eyes. There was a strange calm on her face as if all her feelings had died.

Harshita had come to take Archana and Dhruv to Singapore. Dhruv was now a nine-year-old boy. When Archana sat in the flight having said her goodbyes to Sudha and Govind, who had come to see her off, she thought she would never ever be able to forget the experience of seeing those bodies the first time…and the sight of the bodies… Deepika seemed to be letting out a soundless scream. She felt that scream would follow her and chase her everywhere and continuously point out her failure as a mother.

The plane took off. Down below, the sea that held their ashes lay a poisonous blue.

The Paperboat Maker

Stella filed the report in a nice blue plastic folder and came and stood beside Sudha, who was looking out of the window. There was a breeze blowing through the coconut palms and the palmyras. The rain had stopped. A sparrow flew in and sat on a palm frond. That prompted a certain chain of thought and Stella sang '*Thennangkeetru oonjalile* [Swinging on the palm frond]', softly, under her breath.

'Hey, this is an old song! How do you know it?' Sudha asked in surprise.

'Can music be pigeonholed as old?' said Stella, walking towards the kitchen while continuing to sing. By the time she came to the end of the song with '*Than pettai thunaiyai thedudhu* [It looks around for its female partner]', she had filled the electric kettle with water, pressed the button and kept two ceramic cups and cinnamon teabags ready. Sudha drank only that every evening. Sometimes Stella would join her. Otherwise she would sling her handbag on her shoulder and leave.

On that day work was not over as yet. That explained the two cups. Standing in the kitchen, Stella said, 'Sudhamma, please go through the report once.'

Just then the button of the kettle popped out.

When the teabags were placed in the cups and boiling water was poured on them, there arose a fragrance of cinnamon.

She took the two cups and placed them on the table. 'At least this report will drill some sense into that Mr Sundarlal's head.'

'Can't say, Stella. Once suspicion sets in, it doesn't go away that easily.'

They sipped their tea. This was not the first case of its kind to come to Sudha's detective firm. Many such cases had come her way – a wife who wanted her husband shadowed, a man who was suspicious of his wife, a businessman who wished to have his potential partner discreetly vetted, a prospective groom who required some investigation before the wedding, etc. She was the only woman in this field. Other incidents had followed since the time she had quite accidentally decided to shadow a girl when she was in college, and then it had become her profession. Her scientist husband, Narendra Gupta, and her daughter, Aruna, had accepted it. She worked from home. She had a teacher who taught her the trade in a systematic way. Vidyasagar Rawte. Everyone had heard of him. He was so astute that he was even able to tell when the Mysore Café's vadas had shrunk a little in size. He would know about the first ever murder in Matunga. He also knew how to hold a magnifying glass and pretend to be a detective looking for clues in order to make his granddaughter laugh.

Chellammal used her keys to get in. Before going to the kitchen to see to the evening meal, she came towards them.

'What happened, Chellamma? Your face looks wilted.'

'Yes,' she said wearily and sat down.

'What is it? Knee pain?'

'Who knows what other aches and pains are going to be visited on me!'

Stella got up and asked, 'Shall I bring some tea?'

'Stella, not that cinnamon tea!'

'No aunty, I'll make some ginger tea,' Stella said.

She made the tea and brought it. After taking a sip, Chellammal said, 'There is a marriage proposal for Mallika.'

Mallika was Chellammal's daughter. She worked as a schoolteacher. After her husband's death Chellammal had cooked in people's homes and raised her daughter single-handed. She had been working in Sudha's house since the time Aruna was born. Sudha and her husband had taken the responsibility of financing Mallika's education.

'That is good news. But why is your face so downcast? How is the groom?'

'Everybody says that he is a good boy. He works in a call centre. He is from a family like ours. He too is from Mumbai.'

'Where in Mumbai?'

'Dharavi. Now they've bought a house in Chunabhatti but they've not moved there yet.'

'Then what is wrong, Chellamma?'

'Somehow I feel that the boy is not quite right.'

'Why?'

'I believe he says he does not like rituals and such things.'

'Well, doesn't that count among the five deadly sins for you?'

'Besides, I believe he writes poetry!'

'You're saying that as if he has some contagious disease.'

'And he writes in Tamil.'

'That is indeed a fatal disease!'

'Go on, Sudhamma, don't joke about this! Will a man who writes poetry be...normal?'

'Chellamma, what era are you living in? Who does not write poetry? Didn't Bharathiyar write poetry? Then...'

'Sudhamma, that is all very well. Will he look after his wife properly? Or will she also have to suffer as Bharathi's wife Chellammal did?'

'Aiyyo! Chellamma...'

'He also runs some literary magazine or something... It is called coconut tree or palmyra tree or...'

'*Thennanthoppu* – Coconut Grove,' Stella interrupted. 'Is that his? Good magazine,' she said.

As Sudha had grown up in Mumbai, her Tamil was rather rusty. Stella's father was a great lover of Tamil. He was very involved with all of the Tamil Sangam's activities. Stella too was well versed in Tamil literature.

As Chellammal sipped her tea she said, 'Sudhamma, please make some enquiries about the boy. Who else do I have? I'll pay you your fee for this.'

Shocked, Sudha looked at her.

'What are you saying, Chellamma?'

'Like what you do for others...'

Stella began to laugh.

'Don't laugh!' said Chellammal with a stern look. 'What is there to laugh in this? I want a report on that boy.'

Sudha calmed her down saying, 'OK Chellamma,

we'll do that. Mallika is like a daughter of this house. Don't talk nonsense about fees and such stuff.'

Chellammal looked a little mollified.

'What is the boy's name?'

'Singaravelu Arumugam,' Stella said at once.

'Wow, how did you know that?'

'That magazine – the name is given there. His pen name is Amalan.'

'OK Chellamma, it looks like Stella herself will be able to write the report.'

'No, no, Sudhamma, you make proper enquiries. He might be one of those literature-crazy characters. If he were like everyone else, there would be no worries.'

After a short silence, 'Sudhamma, another thing. During a conversation he mentioned in passing, "My father passed away when I was ten years old."'

'So what, Chellamma?'

'He has a fifteen-year-old sister. Where did she come from? His mother is a teacher. Who knows what that is all about? I have struggled alone to bring up my daughter. Shouldn't she get married into a good family?'

'Yes. We shall see. Don't worry, I'll make enquiries.'

Only after that did Chellammal achieve the right frame of mind to go in and start the cooking.

Stella opened a file titled 'Singaravelu Arumugam (Amalan)' and then left for the day.

~

The next day Stella brought some of her copies of *Thennanthoppu* magazine to show Sudha. Sudha did not understand much of it. Stella placed them in the file.

'Stella, phone Sundarlal's secretary and send that report.'

'I'll do it right away.'

Once that was done, she looked at the diary to see what Sudha had to do next.

'Sudhamma, don't we have to start Chellamma's work?'

'Oh, I completely forgot! Where shall we begin,

Stella? Shall we make enquiries at the call centre?'

'We can do that too, Sudhamma. Chellammal leaves at one after doing the morning's cooking. Then she comes back only in the evening. So you could call up Mr Singaravelu on some pretext or the other, invite him over and talk to him.'

'See if the magazine carries a telephone number.'

'There is a mobile phone number. I'll give it to you,' she said and, writing down the number, stuck it on the file and put it in front of Sudha. She pressed the digits and handed the mobile to Sudha. Then she sat in front of the computer and started looking through the day's mail.

When the call was answered at the other end Sudha said in a businesslike manner, in English, 'Hello! May I speak to Mr Singaravelu?'

'Yes, speaking,' was the reply.

She opened the file to make sure of the name of the magazine.

'You're running a Tamil magazine called *Thennanthoppu*, right?'

'Yes madam,' came the slightly surprised reply.

'I'd like to make a donation; it's a good magazine.'

'Thank you, madam. Which section do you like? You have not mentioned your name. You could send it as a cheque or I could come in person and collect it.'

'My name is Sudha Gupta. I like the magazine in general. Can you come after one o'clock?'

'I can, madam. I work in a call centre, so I only work nights. Please give me the address.'

She gave him the address and he said, 'I'll come, madam,' in Tamil and disconnected the phone.

She attended to all urgent business, fixed dates for certain meetings and worked out how the problems created by certain reports could be sorted out. Before she could even ask for it, Stella had printed out some details and placed them in front of her.

Meanwhile, Malu, who was the housemaid, came and did her work and left. Chellammal had come in and started cooking. Sudha always ate lunch with Stella, who invariably brought something in her tiffin box and shared it.

Chellammal would finish cooking and take something in a lunch box for herself. Only rarely did she sit down with Sudha and Stella for lunch.

That day too she had finished cooking, and set the table with water to drink, pickles, salt and yoghurt. She had also put the food in thermal containers and placed them on the table along with serving spoons.

Chellammal left saying, 'Sudhamma, I am leaving now. Today is my husband's death anniversary. I made some paruppu payasam and vadai. I have kept them on the table as well, please eat them.'

~

At exactly one-thirty the doorbell rang. As Stella was busy with her work, Sudha opened the door herself.

A young man was standing at the door. He had a bag in his hand. His hair was pressed down neatly. Brilliant eyes and an open smile.

'I am Singaravelu.'

'Come in, come in.'

She asked him to sit down and brought him a glass of water and placed it before him. He drank the water and placed the glass on the three-legged stool. Then he opened his bag and took out some magazines.

'Have you seen our latest issues, madam?'

As she glanced through them she asked, 'Since when have you been in Mumbai?' He did not notice that there was a digital recorder under the stool.

When he was about to leave after some minutes of conversation, she gave him a cheque for the magazine and said, 'Why don't you stay for lunch?' Without any sign of fuss he agreed. He asked her where the washroom was and washed his hands and came back.

Stella quietly slipped out and laid another plate on the table. Sudha introduced her to Singaravelu. They sat down to lunch.

As they ate, he told them about his call centre job. He asked Stella about her work. She told him that she helped Sudha with her private enterprise.

Sudha indicated that her work had something to do with the stock market. He spoke in an easy manner about his work and his mother. He told them about his younger sister. 'Right now her only work is in front of a mirror!' he said and laughed.

When Stella asked about one of his poems, he asked her, surprised, 'Do you read all that?'

Softly she asked him, 'When you say, "He opened her", doesn't the man appear dominant even during their coming together?'

'Why do you think so?'

'Balachander in his movies shows the coming together of a man and a woman with the image of the cover being removed from the tanpura. This is the same as that. A very simplistic symbolism. She is an instrument. He is going to play her. She becomes an object that he uses, isn't that so?'

He gave her a quick, piercing look and said, 'Never thought of it that way. But what you say seems quite appropriate.'

Sudha only understood their conversation in general but as she did not know anything about poetry she did not interrupt.

Singaravelu left at two-thirty.

'Do come and see us often,' said Sudha. 'If you come at this time I am relatively free.'

'Definitely,' he said and took their leave.

Stella went in and began to work.

'Stella, don't you think he's a rather different kind of person?'

'Why, because he writes poetry?'

'No. After he finished his lunch, he took his plate in and washed it, did you notice that?'

'Hmm...'

'Normally men do not do things like that. His mother is a teacher. She is a working woman. Therefore he seems to be a very responsible kind of man.'

'Hmm...'

'There is no need to transcribe that recording now. We can do it all at the same time. Just feed it into the computer for now.'

'OK Sudhamma.'

'*Chhamak chhallo!*' the phone sang.

'Stella, please, I don't want all these ringtones

on my phone,' she said as she answered the phone.

'May I speak to Sudha Gupta?'

'This is Sudha Gupta speaking.'

'My name is Puja Advani. Does your agency accept the job of tailing someone?'

'That depends on who has to be tailed and where. The fee for doing it will also depend on those things.'

'This is a very private matter. Therefore...'

'Every case that comes to me is a private matter.'

'No, it is not like that. My husband Tarak Advani comes home very late at night.'

'Since when?'

'Since two years.'

'You didn't make any enquiries about it all this while?'

'No. He works in Dubai. He comes here only once every six months. So in the beginning I did not pay much attention. But this happens every time he is here.'

'Does he have any bad habits?'

'Bad habits...meaning?'

'Going to bars, gambling, such things...'

'Oh no, he is a very good man.'

'Then?'

'I looked at the call log on his phone. He calls a certain number at night even from Dubai.'

'Whose number is it?'

'I don't know. When I called that number a girl picked up. I immediately disconnected the phone.'

'You seem to know everything already!'

'No. I don't know where he goes at night.'

'Well, how many days do you want us to follow him?'

'Four days.'

'Is he now in Mumbai?'

'Yes, and he said that he is going out tonight as well.'

'A night job. Therefore it will cost you a thousand rupees a night. Plus other expenses. And also my fee. Where do you live?'

'Napean Sea Road, Rainbow Apartments. I accept your conditions. May I come to see you today?'

'Just a minute,' Sudha said and was about to

pick up her diary when Stella wrote '5 p.m.' and showed it to her.

'You may come at five o'clock.'

'OK. Thanks.'

As soon as she put down the mobile phone, Stella made a note of the name and the number. She sent an SMS saying, 'Please pay advance amount for four days.' She attached their address and the route to get there.

'Stella, can you stay for a bit? Or do you have something else to do?'

'I can stay, Sudhamma.'

'Shall we call Sundar for the night job? Or should we tell Pradeep?'

'This is a delicate matter. There should be no untoward outcome. Shall we ask Peter?'

'Actually, Ismail too is good at handling such matters.'

'I just thought that since Peter lives in Colaba, it'll be convenient for him.'

'That's true.'

Sudha liked every job to begin immediately. So Stella got in touch with Peter straight away. She told him that there might be a job that night and gave him the details. She said she would confirm it in a short while.

Puja Advani came at the appointed time. She had a majestic and imposing personality but she was not overbearing. She spoke to them in an easy, friendly manner. In a very disarming fashion she told them about how she had moved up in life from humble Cheeta Camp to Napean Sea Road. She spoke highly of her husband, Tarak Advani. He was a good man. She felt that he could have become entangled in some difficulty. He had not changed in the way he behaved towards her. But she sensed a slight distance between them. This might be due to that girl, she felt. Their children had grown up, and they now lived in Canada and the US.

She gave them two numbers that he was constantly in touch with. She said they were the mobile phone numbers of that girl. When she called the second number, a man had answered. She had cut off the connection immediately, without saying anything. She reminded them that her husband was going out that day as well and had said that he would leave around 7.30 p.m.

She had brought the advance amount in cash. She gave that to Sudha and took her leave. When Stella asked if she could be dropped off at Bandra, she graciously agreed to give her a lift.

Stella texted Peter the details of that evening's job as she left.

Chellammal too left shortly after they did. After everyone had left, Sudha went and sat down on the sofa in the living room. On the round centre table in front of her was the sheet of paper on which Puja had written the two numbers.

She thought, why not try calling these numbers, and called the first one.

'Hello, mummy is not here. She has gone out. Who is this?' asked a girl's voice in Hindi. The way she asked, *'Aap kaun?'* sounded like she was a rather young girl.

Sudha disconnected the call. She called the second number. On the mobile's screen appeared the words 'Dialling Singaravelu'. Before she could disconnect, 'Hello Sudha madam. What news?' said Singaravelu's voice.

'Sorry. I pressed your number by mistake.' Then she mentioned the other number and said that she had been trying to get through to that number.

'That's my amma's number, madam! How do you know her?'

'Sorry Velu. Somebody gave it to me by mistake.'

'Never mind, madam. Goodnight.'

~

The next day when Stella came in Sudha said, 'It looks like that report for Chellammal is not going to be easy.'

'Why? Because the number Puja Advani gave is Singaravelu's, isn't it?'

'That's amazing! How did you know?'

'Elementary, Sudhamma! I entered his number into your mobile. When Mrs Advani wrote down the two numbers I already knew that the second one was the number that I'd saved on your phone.

You were unusually tired yesterday. Otherwise when a number is dialled it is normally imprinted in your mind like a photograph. Don't you think I must have acquired at least five per cent of your observation powers?'

Sudha laughed.

Stella put away her handbag and sat down saying, 'It is because I saw the number that I decided to go with her.'

'Right, what happened on the way?'

'She is really a very good person. When they were in Cheeta Camp, he was the municipal corporator of Trombay, Mankhurd area. He made a very good name for himself. He helped solve the problems of many people. Singaravelu's father had a small shop. Mr Advani helped him set up a little tea stall within the shop. At that time Singaravelu's mother was not a teacher. I chatted with her casually and managed to get this information.'

'He helped them. Why does he have to suddenly establish contact with them now?'

'That is what we need to know.'

'Has Peter sent in his report?'

'He sent it early this morning. Last night he sent me an SMS.'

'What about?'

'That his work was over by 11.30 p.m.'

'Where did he go?'

'He asked the neighbours about the house Mr Tarak Advani entered in Dharavi. They told him that it was the house of a teacher and that she had a son called Singaravelu and a daughter called Sunaina.'

'Sunaina? That is not a Tamil name.'

'It is not. It is Mr Advani's mother's name, I found that out from Google.'

'What?!'

'Yes. Why does she have that name? What is the connection? I just cannot figure it out.'

'This is like a monster coming out when all one wanted to do was dig a well!'

'We have not even dug a well. But the monster is here already,' Stella said and laughed.

They read Peter's report together.

I started my duty at 7.30 p.m. (In fact at 6.30 – as one did not know when the particular individual would actually leave, I got there as early as 6.30 p.m.) When Mr Advani sat in the car and the driver started it, I began following them on my motorbike. (They own two cars. The lady of the house had gone out in one car. I learnt that from the watchman of the building. Hers is a new Fiat. Her driver is a man from Uttar Pradesh named Sreekant. Mr Advani's car is a Maruti 1000. His driver is Tamil. Name: Anbazhagan.) As they were leaving I heard him say to the driver, 'To Dharavi. By the Sea Link.' As motorbikes are not allowed on the Sea Link, after we came to Warden Road, Haji Ali, and they turned towards the Sea Link, I went from Worli to Bandra by Tulsipipe Road and waited for them at the turn to the highway. As soon as their car got into Bandra from the Sea Link I began following them again. There was very heavy traffic at that time. The car turned to the right from Bandra, entered a narrow street in Dharavi and stopped outside a house. It was 9 p.m. Mr Advani went into the house. When I struck up a casual conversation with the paanwala and the people standing nearby, I found out that she is a teacher in a school in Wadala. Name: Malarvizhi. The teacher has a son. Name: Singaravelu Arumugam. (Singaravelu was the name of a late Communist leader. The teacher's late husband was an ardent supporter of left-wing parties. Husband's name: Arumugam.) The teacher has a daughter as well. Name: Sunaina. The son works in a call centre. He is also studying to complete his MA degree privately. He is passionate about Tamil. He publishes a Tamil magazine. Name: Thennanthoppu. He runs a library for the children in Dharavi. He also gives computer lessons. For many years he used to own a TVS Scooty to go around. He has just bought himself a red Bajaj Kristal. It was parked in a corner by the side of the house. The daughter is in the tenth standard. She goes to classes at Mahesh Tutorials. She came home an hour after Mr Advani went in.

Mr Advani stayed for exactly half an hour after she reached home. It was 10 p.m. when Mr Advani stepped out. The teacher and her son came out with smiling faces to see him off. Mr Advani's face was beaming. He came and sat in the car and took their leave, waving from the car. The teacher's son too left at the same time.

The car went back the way it had come. I took the Mahim Tulsipipe Road and again waited for them in Worli. Then the car went to Napean Sea Road. It was 11 p.m. by then. When I got to Colaba it was 11.30 p.m.

I have attached a scanned copy of the petrol bill and a copy of the bill at the dosa and tea shop (onion rava dosa with three different chutneys, the taste lingers still on the tip of my tongue).

P.S.: Stella, Sudha ma'am, what can I do if there are so many unpronounceable Tamil names in just a single case? I had to struggle really hard. You fold your tongue and the word comes from somewhere inside the throat. That sound for which you use 'zh' in English, I don't think I can ever manage to say it. But I am always ready to eat onion rava dosa!

'The usual complete report from Peter. Does he still have to follow him for another three days?'

'Definitely. We have nothing substantial in hand as yet, Stella.'

The report that came from Peter after three days was very clear. It said that from the first day through the entire four-day period, Mr Advani visited the same house in Dharavi.

~

Deciding what to do next was a rather tricky problem. Meanwhile, Singaravelu visited them a few times. He was very lively and friendly in his conversation. 'Ma'am, you don't have to address me in the respectful form of "vanga", "ponga", and so on. After all, I am just a young man,' he said one day to Sudha. Once his mother called and said that Singaravelu had told her a lot about Sudha and she invited Sudha to come and visit her sometime. Meanwhile, Chellammal kept pushing her, asking if she had found out everything about the family.

After thinking a great deal about it Sudha decided to go and see Malarvizhi. It was a holiday for Malarvizhi. It was also not a day of heavy downpours; it had rained only intermittently. She chose a day when she knew Singaravelu would not be home. Malarvizhi was very natural and open about herself and Sudha felt pangs of guilt about recording the conversation with the digital recorder concealed in her purse. She felt she was betraying a friend. But she had to do it.

When she came back, she played some parts for Stella.

Come, come, Sudhamma. Aiyyo, I am so happy that you're here. Please sit on the chair. I'll put your umbrella here. My son has told me a lot about you. He has gone to Vasai on some work. Sunaina has a special class today.

[Someone: Teacheramma, give me an umbrella, please. When I left home there was no rain. Now it has started. Shall I take this one here?

Aiyyo, that is my guest's umbrella. Take this one.]

Come, Sudhamma, let us eat and talk. Since it is a holiday, I had time to make egg curry. I have made it with coconut milk. Our neighbour got some fried fish from Koliwada. Do you like fish? There's also a snake-gourd poriyal.

...

Malarvizhi, Singaravelu has told me a lot about you. About your being a teacher, his running a magazine, the respect that your neighbours have for you – all this tells me that you're an amazing person. Tell me about yourself. Don't think that I am doing this like an interview. I'd like to know, that is all.

Why should I not tell you, Sudhamma? I somehow feel very close to you. I don't know why. It has been a long while since I opened my heart to anyone, Sudhamma...

Where shall I begin? Here in this photograph is my husband. He was related to me. A distant cousin. He had studied only up to the tenth standard. The conditions in his family were not very good, poor man. He could not study any further. He was very hard-working. He did the usual farm jobs. I studied up to plus two. I wanted to continue my studies. But it was the same with my family – not enough resources. Appa fell ill. I was the last child. My family felt that they should get me married so they could get over with their responsibilities. People from my husband's family came to ask for a bride. Although he was not educated, I liked his nature. I agreed. Next year our son was born. My husband liked the Communist ideology. He would talk a lot about such issues. That is why we named our son Singaravelu. You know of Singaravelu, don't you?

The Paperboat Maker

When Thambi was just four we moved here. Agricultural work had become unviable. We came here with a distant relative. But he abandoned us in a pavement hut in Chembur. Soon after that, through someone else, we met a good man called Tarak Advani. Tarak saheb was the municipal corporator in Cheeta Camp, Trombay area. He is like an elder brother to me. Why, I could even say he is like a father to me! He made it possible for us to live in Cheeta Camp. He got my husband a licence to set up a kiosk with a tea-vending outlet. Not just that. He urged me to study further. I began to study for a BA degree. Just when I had completed my BA and joined a teacher's training course, Tarak saheb went off to Dubai. One day I don't know what happened. I was just leaving when my husband, who had gone to the shop early in the morning, said, 'Malar, something is wrong with me.' I said, 'Did you listen to me when I said don't eat chhole at night? Whole chickpeas are not good at night but do you listen? It is gas!' I put down my bag and books and went and got some omam and venthiyam. When I came back, he was sitting on the chair, clutching his chest. When he saw me, he lifted his hand towards me, and then his hand fell... Ahhh...

Don't cry, Malar. Shall I bring you some water?

Forgive me, Sudhamma. It has been seventeen years since he passed away. But he is still there in my heart. Never a harsh word; never any regrets. He did not even chew paan...

Sunaina...

That is another story. It is not a good story. But Sunaina came as a gift. My son adores her...

I told you that Tarak saheb was in Dubai when my husband passed away, didn't I? He had a brother called Vinay Advani. He was the one who stood by us at that time. He told me that he would buy the kiosk and the tea stall. He wanted to set up a restaurant in its place. But I did not have the heart to do that, so I employed a person and continued running them.. Vinay Advani was not like his brother. He was not friendly with everyone. But he used to often come to my house. Perhaps because we were a family his brother supported...

I understand, Malar. You don't have to tell me.

No, Sudhamma, I'll tell you. My heart is full and

overflowing today. Wait, Sudhamma, I'll bring some water.

When I think about it, I get choked. I was all alone, Sudhamma, and at one point I softened towards him. Only when suddenly something began to grow inside me did I come to my senses. He said, 'We don't want to be here. We'll go some place else.' He had some standing in Dharavi. So we took a place here on rent and moved. From here, my son went to school in Chembur. He bought the shop and gave me the money. When he came after two days I cooked him a feast. He liked only mutton curry. He ate well that morning and left. That was it, he did not come back. However many times I tried calling him, he did not answer. A three-month foetus in my womb! Whom could I speak to, where could I go? There was a lady called Saraswati who lived next door. I used to call her 'aya'. I called her over and wailed, 'Aya, this is what happened. Tell me a way of getting rid of it.' She said she would.

I did not know that at some point during our conversation my son had returned from school. Later, when I placed a plate in front of him and served him some rice, he caught hold of my hand and said, 'Amma!' His eyes were brimming with tears. I panicked and asked him what it was.

'Amma, don't do anything to the baby,' he said. I was totally shaken up. He was not yet twelve then. Perhaps children who see many different things around them get that way, or was he a truly exceptional child? I don't know, Sudhamma. He spoke to me then like an adult. I took both his hands and placed them on my face and heart. I wept. 'Dei, you're not my son. You're my father. You're god, my father,' I said and cried.

I sold the few bits of jewellery I had. With that, and with part of the money from selling the shop, I got this place with Saraswati aya's help. I put the remaining money in the bank. My education was interrupted for a whole year. Sunaina was born. Within a week Tarak saheb was there; he had asked around and managed to find out where we were. When he saw the baby he was shocked. I did not hide anything from him. He told me to name her after his mother. Even now, Sunaina calls him 'taoji'. He comes every now and then but frequently talks on the phone with us. He is bearing all of Sunaina's educational expenses. If I try to tell him not to do it, he won't hear of it. It is only at his urging that Velu has now started working on his MA. Velu runs a library for the children who live around here and also holds computer classes for them. He takes the kids out on picnics.

Velu has a very good heart.

He is not just my son, Sudhamma, he is my friend. He thinks the world of his little sister. For the last two years Tarak saheb has been trying to persuade us to allow his family to adopt Sunaina. I believe his brother died of cancer. He had no children. When Tarak saheb told his brother's wife about Sunaina, she began pleading with him to get Sunaina, saying that she wanted to immediately adopt her. Velu totally refused. Sunaina too said, 'No way, taoji!' He keeps making phone calls. By the time Sunaina comes back from her tutorials it is usually nine or nine-thirty. So whenever he visits us, he waits till then and leaves only after seeing her and speaking to her. I believe Sunaina looks just like his mother.

~

When they had finished listening, Stella brought out the printed sheets with the transcripts of the conversations they had had with Singaravelu every time he visited. She had recorded them and entered the transcripts into the computer.

From the first recording:

Singaravelu Arumugam (S.A.): *We came to Bombay when I was just four years old. We were living in Cheeta Camp. Appa died when I was ten. We had to struggle a lot. Memories of appa are very hazy in my mind. Only his voice resounds in my memory as clear as a bronze bell. It was only after I grew up that I looked at all the books in his trunk. He too was interested in literature. The books of poetry of Bharathiyar and Bharathidasan – he had covered those with clear plastic covers. Pudumaipitthan and Ku Azhagiriswamy, he had covered with thick sheets of paper. Inside he had written his name and the date showing when they had been bought. He had bound together many copies of* Thamarai *magazine. The receipts of purchase of some of the books were still there. I kept touching those receipts. I felt that I was actually touching him.*

From the second recording:

S.A.: *Initially, I studied in a municipal school where the medium of instruction was Tamil. As that was not very good, they put me in an English medium school. The Star English High School there came up only later, in 1998. So they put me in OLPS School in Chembur. Most of the people in Cheeta Camp were Tamils. There was a Tamil teacher called Ismail there. He and appa taught me Tamil. Ismail sir was a good singer. He was an old man. When he and appa sang old Tamil film songs, everyone would crowd around them. Appa could even sing songs that were from before his time because of his friendship with Ismail sir. Ismail sir would start singing* 'Odam nathiyinile...' [A boat on the river ...] *and appa would join in. Ismail sir would begin the next song,* 'Amaithiyana nathiyinile odum odam...' [The boat moving on the quietly flowing river...] *as well. A song that they both liked was* 'Indru poy, nalai vaarai...' [Leave the battlefield today, come tomorrow...] *a song from the film* Sampurna Ramayanam. *Ismail sir would marvel at the acting of T.K. Bhagavathi.*

With poignant emotion Ismail sir would even sing songs meant for a female voice. He would start, 'Sonnathu neethana...' [Did you utter those words...] *and continue with the plaintive words, 'Sol, sol, sol, en uyire...'* [Tell me, tell me, tell me my dearest...].

I wrote my first poem at the age of nine.

Stella: *Do you remember it?*

S.A.: *I do, I do. My first poem after all!*

- I told a lie
  My heart is heavy today.

Stella: *So you were lying even then!*

(Laughter)

In the transcript of the third recording, he talked almost exclusively about literature. Therefore nothing in that had been underlined.

From the fourth transcript:

S.A.: *Cheeta Camp was a wonderful place. The people there were very united. Even during the 1992 communal riots there were no disturbances at all over there.*

Sudha: *Then why did you leave Cheeta Camp and go to Dharavi?*

S.A.: *It was only in 1994 that we left Cheeta Camp and went to Dharavi. We thought it would be more convenient there for amma to continue her studies...*

Sudha: *What is your sister studying?*

S.A.: *She is in the tenth standard.*

Sudha: *Your poor appa was not able to see her at all...*

S.A.: *Her father and my father were not the same, madam.*

Sudha: *Meaning?*

S.A.: *After appa passed away, amma had another relationship. That is when my sister was born.*

Stella: *Doesn't your amma try to persuade you to get married?*

S.A.: *She does. But I do not believe in rituals. No dowry in cash or kind. A simple registration ceremony. If she believes in wearing a thali, then I'll tie one. That is all.*

Stella: *What kind of wife do you seek?*

S.A.: *I don't know. I am a little crazy. I keep getting involved in literary activities, a children's library, this, that and the other. Besides, I have started studying for my MA. She should not have any objections to all that.*

Stella: *What will you do for her?*

S.A.: *I'll be a good friend to her. I'll not be the kind of husband who says, 'Bring me a cup of coffee!'*

(Laughter)

Stella: *No falling in love and all that...*

S.A.: *I don't know, perhaps it came and went without my knowing. In the train just the day before yesterday I met someone who was in Cheeta Camp with me. Her name is Usha Rani. She had a three-year-old son and a baby girl of just a year in her arms. 'Velu,' she herself called out and talked to me, 'aren't you married yet?'*

'I have not managed to find a girl yet!' I said and laughed.

'When the girl was right in front of you, you could not see her, could you?' she said.

When I asked her, 'What are you saying?' she replied,

'When I met you once in Chembur Market, after I had finished my tenth standard, I bought you a plastic dil from the shop there, don't you remember?'

'Dil?'

'Yes, a red one, a red heart with an arrow through it.'
I stared, totally perplexed.

'See! I told you what was in my heart but did you understand?'

'Really?'

'Now you ask me, after I have had two children!' she said and gave me an affectionate slap on the cheek (it did hurt a bit!) and left.

(Laughter)

~

The report for Mrs Advani was written and dispatched with a bill for services rendered.

When Chellammal came in, Sudha called her in and gave her all the details and said, 'He is a good boy, Chellamma. You cannot find any fault in him. He is rather dark and our Mallika is very fair, we could say that is a drawback perhaps. But he is in all other ways a very suitable match.'

'What, Sudhamma, how can you say that? The mother's character is not good at all.'

'Sometimes one makes mistakes in life, Chellamma. Don't make too much of that. The young man is a gem. Without your knowledge, I called him here and spoke to him.'

'Really!'

'See, we have recorded everything he said. I'll play it for you if you like. Or read the written report. Stella, bring the report here!'

'Don't, Stella, let it be,' Chellammal refused.

When Sudha tried to explain further with 'He has a very friendly nature, he speaks very freely with everyone', Chellammal countered, 'He probably takes after his mother. Somehow I don't like this. I know Mallika will not agree either. She is also like me. This will not work. I'll tell them the answer is no.'

'Shall I speak to Mallika?'

'No Sudhamma. She is my daughter. I know

her. She has another image in her mind. A handsome, good man...'

'Who is a good man?'

'A man like other men. Will you even consider a man like this for our Aruna?'

'Why do you talk like this, Chellamma? To me, is Mallika different from Aruna? If Aruna likes a man I don't think I'll say no. Leave it, Chellamma! Do what you would like to. I'll not try to persuade you.'

'Are you angry, Sudhamma?'

'Not at all, Chellamma. Have I ever been angry with you?'

Chellammal got up and went into the kitchen.

Stella put the report away in the cupboard and then pulled shut the glass door that separated the office from the passage to the kitchen and the waiting room. When she was sure that Chellammal would not be able to hear what she said, she spoke in a soft, low voice.

'Sudhamma, I like Singaravelu.'

'Does that mean you're going to marry him?' Sudha asked in a jocular manner.

'Why shouldn't I?'

'It looks like you might even tell your appa about this!'

'I've already told him.'

'What? But you didn't tell me! When did you decide this?'

'Even before you went to see his mother. But I didn't tell you. Mallika is also my friend, isn't she? So I thought I should tell you about it only after she and her mother had said no to the match.'

'How did you come to this decision, Stella?'

'Four or five days ago, I went to Dharavi to buy a leather bag. A bout of heavy rain had just stopped. Somewhere in the interior there was an event which I thought I should attend – at least show my face. There, on the way, in a little lane, was the children's library that Velu had talked about. Rainwater had flooded the entrance. Velu was sitting there making paper boats for the ten or so children who were clustered around him. They were sailing them in the water, clapping their hands in glee and having a great time. I was watching all this from a distance. He did not see me. The children were climbing on him and falling all over him and screaming away. He was not in the slightest bit irritated, and he kept smiling all the while. That was when I decided. I told appa almost immediately.'

'What next?'

'I'll ask appa to talk to his mother.'

'You could call him yourself and tell him, wouldn't that be better?'

'I have to find out whether he likes me or not. I wonder what he'll say if he learns about my line of work.'

'Of course he'll like you, Stella. How can anybody not like you? Go on, call him and tell him.'

'Oh no. He knows nothing about love. I'll have to teach him!' said Stella and laughed out loud.

A Meeting on the Andheri Overbridge

Sudha Gupta was rushing to catch the 10.17 Bhayandar fast train. That train would not be very crowded. All the other alternatives were Virar fast trains, and they would be choking with crowds.

Since the Andheri station was being extended and renovated, the place was strewn with debris. Monstrous and destructive dinosaur bulldozers stood ready to flatten everything around them. Sudha entered platform no. 1 with the intention of going up the stairs to the overbridge.

There were continuous announcements on the public address system about the arrivals and departures of trains. The announcements were interspersed with warnings such as 'There are electric cables carrying 25,000 volts above the trains. We request passengers not to travel on the roofs of the trains as it could lead to death.' Other announcements advised passengers not to cross rails on foot, not to spit on platforms, not to bathe oneself or animals on the platform or wash vessels on the platform. Only in Mumbai could one hear such announcements, nowhere else in the world, she felt.

Milling crowds pushed and propelled her up the steps. On the bridge she turned right and was walking towards platform no. 4 when she saw the beggars, the regulars of that area. The man who begged in the name of Allah, the hunchback beggar girl and two others who were blind. At a slight distance was the man who sold soaps and powders claiming they were imported stuff. By his side was a heap of old books. There were some people chatting on their mobile phones, standing around waiting for their friends.

Even before she reached the steps leading down to platform no. 4, she could hear…she could hear musical notes coming from a flute. A beggar who was a regular there played on the flute; he loved songs from the fifties and sixties. He was a fan

A Meeting on the Andheri Overbridge

of Adi Narayana Rao and would always start his playing with '*Kuhu kuhu bole koyaliya*', a song in multiple ragas from the film *Swarna Sundari*. Then he would go on to a film song from Sudhir Phadke's *Bhabhi Ki Chudiyaan* and move on to the notes of '*Jyothi kalash chalke*'. But if he was in a sad frame of mind, he would go to the plaintive strains of '*Chaahunga main tujhe saanj savere*' and melt one's heart just as Mohammed Rafi did singing it. Or Talat Mahmood's song from *Baradari*: '*Tasveer banata hoon, tasveer nahin banti*'. Then Manna Dey, Mukesh – all in that order. If it was the monsoons, he would definitely play '*Pyaar hua ikraar hua*', from the film *Shree 420*, or '*Yeh raat bheegi bheegi*', from the film *Chori Chori*. Sometimes college students would ask him to play Rashid Khan's song '*Aoge jab tum saajana*', from *Jab We Met*.

He had not finished playing his second song. That meant the 10.17 had not yet arrived. She noticed the woman when she was just beginning to climb down the stairs. She could not have been more than sixty. She had spread a clean sheet on the ground and was sitting on it, a small suitcase and handbag by her side. Definitely not a beggar. There was no begging bowl or plate in front of her. Her hair was well combed and she had put it up in a bun at the back and adorned it with a veni of flowers. Still, some people were throwing money on the sheet. She took no notice of that.

Sudha watched her for a moment and then moved on. Perhaps she had come to catch a train going to some other town. She had probably come too early and sat right there since it was very crowded on the platform.

Sudha rushed down the steps just as the Bhayandar fast was pulling in. The flautist was in a good mood and had just begun to play '*Ketaki gulaab juhi champaka vana phoole*', from the movie *Basant Bahar*, a song in which Bhimsen Joshi and Manna Dey were pitted against each other. Just like the song '*Oru naal poduma*' (Will a day be enough?) in *Thiruvilayadal* in which Balamurali and T.M.S. compete. Apparently Manna Dey had had doubts about doing this song, wondering how he could possibly sing in competition with Bhimsen Joshi. And it is said that Bhimsen

A Meeting on the Andheri Overbridge

Joshi had found it difficult to sing as the losing competitor.

On any other day, she would have stopped and listened to the song and taken the next train. But on that day she had some urgent business and was in a hurry. She had to go to Bhayandar and then on to Dahanu. She got into the train and sat down. Exactly when the flute managed to capture Bhimsen Joshi's cascading notes, the train departed.

She had no real detective work in either Bhayandar or Dahanu. The kind of work that regularly came to her involved cases like a wife suspecting her husband or vice versa, business partners wanting to check on each other, or the investigation of a bride or a groom in an arranged marriage. She had acquired a taste for detection when she had shadowed a girl in college. Later she trained under a very well-known detective called Vidyadhar Rawte. Even though Vidyadhar Rawte was getting on in age, he was still highly respected in the profession. He never forgot a face or a name. Once when he was introduced to a very important minister, he whispered in the minister's ear, 'Honourable minister, you should write about your experiences on trains. I'd be very keen to read it.' As a young boy, the minister had been an expert snatcher of women's chains and had frequented local trains and crowded platforms. Even though his name was in many police files, he had never been caught. But Vidyadhar Rawte had never forgotten that. Nor, obviously, had the minister. His face paled and then reddened. He stared angrily and then moved away quickly. Vidyadhar Rawte then said to her, 'Be polite even with chain-snatchers. After twenty years, you'll still be the same, but he would have become a minister!' He had burst into loud laughter. He had had threats from the criminal underworld. A man who was working under the name of Romeo called Vidyadhar Rawte once and said in a threatening tone, 'I am Romeo speaking!' to which he replied, 'Then you better look for a Juliet, I am of no use to you!' and cut the connection. Such were the stories he told. Sudha's scientist husband and their college-going daughter had long since

A Meeting on the Andheri Overbridge

accepted her profession and her use of the house as her office. Though it was not very common for a private detective to work in tandem with the police, Inspector Govind Shelke had been her friend for a great many years. Therefore, whenever he had more work than he could handle, he would give her some.

The Bhayandar job was a rather strange one. She had only taken it up because Malu, who worked in their flat, had importuned her repeatedly. In all general and ladies-only compartments of local trains one can find posters of five or six babas on the walls. Advertisements for making money working from home and for beauty parlours are commonplace in ladies' compartments, as are telephone numbers written on the walls. There was once a declaration – 'Usha is a deceiver. She broke a good young man's heart' – written on the seats and walls with indelible ink that couldn't be erased for a long time. What was the point of the heartbroken man telling women about it? The number of posters advertising babas has increased greatly in recent times. Though the names of the babas may be Hindu or Muslim, the photos are invariably of Shirdi Sai Baba. 'Wherever you may roam, in the end you will have to come here' or 'Don't be deceived by fakes, this is the real baba' and other such competitive slogans. These babas had all sorts of powers and they had solutions for everything. Mental distress, family feuds, promotions at work, bringing down one's enemies, opportunities to go abroad, debt problems, court cases, health problems, problems of sterility, victory in love, opportunities of starring in movies, love spells – there was a whole list of issues for which these babas offered solutions. One particular baba's list included masturbation as one of the problems he could resolve. For all those who have spent their lives depending on their own hand, it must have been a rude shock indeed to see this item on the list.

Malu's problem was not something that belonged to the list. She had gone to a baba to find a remedy for her husband's drinking problem. There the baba gave everyone water that he had consecrated in a silver pot. It was the silver pot that

A Meeting on the Andheri Overbridge

affected her. She told Sudha that fifteen years ago a man calling himself Mahadev Baba had come to Chandrapur. He stayed at their house for two days. And many of their belongings had vanished when he suddenly left one night without telling them. Among those belongings was a silver pot. Malu's mother's name was engraved on it. She wanted the pot back. 'This is the same Mahadev Baba. He has merely changed his name,' she insisted.

'Malu, we could file a complaint against him saying that he is a fake, but how can we get back your silver pot?'

But Malu did not pay any heed. She was adamant. 'It is my mother's. Please get it for me, aunty.' Hence the journey to retrieve that silver pot.

Her work at Dahanu was connected to Govind Shelke's wife, Meenabai. Meenabai was an Adivasi. She and Govind Shelke had fallen in love and got married. She did some social work for the local Adivasi women in Dahanu. There was a government-aided school in that area run by a couple. Many Adivasi girls of those parts attended the school. When two of those girls began to protest that they did not want to go to school, it was after repeated questioning by their parents and one of the girls in Meenabai's social welfare unit that the truth emerged. When the two girls, aged fourteen and sixteen, reached school, their attendance was registered and they were then sent off to work in the house of a couple, which was in the same compound. There, they had to sweep, swab, wash the dishes, cook and do everything else. Not just that, they even had to give oil massages to the couple. The girls were afraid that this would make them vulnerable to abuse of other sorts. They could not tell anybody – the entire school administration was privy to this. If they refused to do the work, they would be threatened and beaten up. The girls wanted to study. They had dreams of acquiring an education and getting big jobs. They cried and said they hated doing housework and those other things and not being allowed to study.

Meenabai wanted to look into this. Before complaining to the higher authorities and the police, she felt that they should investigate the matter thoroughly and prepare a report. So she

A Meeting on the Andheri Overbridge

had sought Sudha's help. They had arranged to meet at Dahanu.

As the train pulled up at the Bhayandar station, inside it announcements in three languages could be heard:

Pudil station Bhayandar
Agala station Bhayandar
Next station Bhayandar

~

The work at Bhayandar got done much sooner than expected. Malu was waiting for her outside the station. They got into an autorickshaw. Sudha had contacted the baba by calling the number given on the poster and fixing up a meeting.

The baba's hirsute face with beard and moustache wore a look of tender sympathy. His hand was permanently held up in a gesture of blessing. *'Sala, thoths aahe, jo Chandrapurla aala hota,'* Mala muttered, telling her that it was the same wretch who had come to Chandrapur.

They paid their respects to him and sat down. Sudha immediately told him about her profession and also gave the name of Govind Shelke. The blessing hand came down and the people around the baba stood sharp in anticipation of his command.

'Is there any problem with a case? We can solve it!' the baba said.

'I need to talk to you alone,' she said in a very respectful manner.

The baba asked the others to leave.

'Baba, have you travelled a great deal and been to many places?'

'This body roams around many places. Does a body stay in just one place?'

'Did this body go to Chandrapur about ten to fifteen years ago?'

'It could have. I don't remember. Many towns. Many places. But my soul rests at His Feet,' he said, pointing to the roof above.

'This girl tells me that you were in Chandrapur.'

'Could have been,' he said and looked at Malu.

'You stayed at their house.'

A Meeting on the Andheri Overbridge

'May have.'

'After you left, it was discovered that many of their puja vessels were gone.'

'Is that so? Everything is His leela, His sport,' he said and glared at Malu.

'If the baba does not mind, may I please hold your silver pot in my hands?'

'It is a consecrated pot. If you hold it with the wrong intentions, it will burn your hands to cinders.'

'No wrong intentions at all, babaji. I just want to see it. That is all,' she said. Just then her mobile phone rang. 'Just a minute,' she said and answered the phone. 'Oh, Inspector Shelke? I am here in Bhayandar. I have come to see Shankar Baba...' she said loudly and then put the phone back into the handbag.

'You may handle this with devotion,' the baba said and held out the pot. When she took it in her hands she saw engraved on it 'Sakkubai' in Marathi script. *'Maaja aayicha naav,'* Malu said in a whisper, confirming it was her mother's name.

'Please give this pot to her with your blessings.

This is her mother's name on it,' she said, pointing to the letters engraved on the pot.

After some thought, the baba called one of his helpers and told him to pour the water in the pot into another pot and then proffered it to Sudha. 'This was given to me by one of my devotees. The baba who visited her house must have been a *dhongi* baba, a fake one. I don't have the heart to refuse since you ask for it with such devotion. The hearts of all babas are made of wax, just wax,' he said and gave the pot to her. He touched them both on their heads and blessed them. 'He did not touch my head, he rapped my head with his knuckles,' Malu told Sudha when they came out.

Malu put the silver pot into a bag and left saying, 'Thanks, aunty.' Sudha went to the station to take the train to Dahanu.

Just as she and Meenabai had expected, it was difficult to make enquiries in Dahanu. When she managed to find some excuse to question people at the school, they showed her the attendance register to prove that the two girls had actually attended school. The two girls were very frightened. The

A Meeting on the Andheri Overbridge

other children in the school refused to speak. When they spoke to Shelke and asked him to find out what the couple had been doing before they came here, the information arrived within an hour. They had run a school near Sawantwadi and had been thrown out because of similar behaviour, but there was no proper proof. While they were wondering if she could proceed to question the couple just on the basis of that information, a teacher who had recently joined the school called Meenabai on her mobile phone. She too had been harassed by the couple in other ways. She was an Adivasi.

They discussed how the teacher could help. Together they gently persuaded the two girls to speak about what had happened and recorded their testimony. It was decided that the girls would go to school for the next two days and the teacher who had come forward to help would secretly record on her mobile phone their going to the other side of the compound and, if possible, their doing work in the house. Without that evidence they felt it would not be possible to take any further action. The necessary evidence could be collected in two or three days and reported to the higher authorities and the police.

By the time all this was done it was six o'clock. Sudha was tired. In the train, she sat with her feet on the seat opposite her and dozed off till she reached Andheri station. She went up the stairs and was turning left on the overbridge when she was taken aback by what she saw.

The woman she had seen in the morning was still sitting in the same place. The money that people had flung at her in coins and notes remained on the sheet.

Sudha did not have the heart to just keep going. She slowly walked towards the woman.

'Mausi, I saw you this morning as well. It is eight now and you're still here. What's the matter?' Sudha asked her.

'Please leave. Nothing's the matter.'

'No, mausi. This is not a good place to be. Even the beggars are leaving. What is the matter, tell me please.'

A Meeting on the Andheri Overbridge

Keeping her head bent, the woman refused to speak.

'Mausi, tell me what it is. I'll do my best to help. I cannot leave you like this. If you remain obstinate, I'll have to call the police. Then everything will become unpleasant.'

On hearing the mention of police, the woman said, 'No, don't call the police. I'll leave.' Having said that, she got up, picked up the money on the sheet and put it in the begging mug of the blind beggar who had still not left. She then began to fold the sheet.

'I'll leave. You should too,' she told Sudha.

'I did not mention the word police because I wanted you to get up. I said it because I am genuinely worried about you. Where is your house?'

'Don't bother the life out of me. I don't have a home.'

'OK, you don't have a home. There is a women's hostel close by. Women who've had to leave home and go away in a hurry can stay there for two or three days. You'll get a room there. My friend is the director. Will you go there? You can go now and get some sleep. I'll talk to you tomorrow morning. I am not pressuring you to do anything. You're elderly. Please heed what I'm saying.'

'All right. I'll go to the hostel.'

'Your name?'

'Sandhyabai.'

'Age?'

'Sixty.'

She at once spoke to Mary. When she gave her the details, Mary agreed to give Sandhyabai a room to stay.

She walked down the stairs with Sandhyabai and caught an autorickshaw. The hostel was on her way home. She told the driver that there would be a wait of about ten minutes on the way and he agreed. They got into the auto.

Once they reached the hostel they went in and asked for Mary, who was upstairs. She came down immediately and got a girl to note down the details in the register. Once that was done, she unlocked a room and turned on the light.

A Meeting on the Andheri Overbridge

A small room. A bed with a blue and yellow sheet on the mattress. A table with a bottle of water and a glass on it.

Sandhyabai walked in, put down her little suitcase and looked up at Mary and Sudha. Her face, for the first time, brightened a little. She put her palms together and said, 'Dhanyavaad.'

The autorickshaw driver was honking away outside telling her to hurry.

'I'll see you tomorrow morning, mausi,' Sudha said and, taking leave of Mary, she walked out.

~

The next morning Sudha reached the hostel around ten. When she knocked on Sandhyabai's door, she saw that Sandhyabai was ready, having had a bath and changed her clothes. After asking her if she wanted to extend her stay there for two more days, Sudha went to see Mary. Mary agreed to the extension and made the necessary arrangements.

Sudha went back to the room and asked, 'Mausi, shall we leave?'

'Where to?'

'My place. We will be able to talk there in quiet surroundings. Have you had breakfast?'

'No.'

'OK, let's go.'

As soon as they sat in the car, she drove them to the Seven Bungalows neighbourhood and parked at the entrance to Swadesh Hotel. It was not very crowded. They sat in the corner at a table for two.

'Mausi, what shall I order?'

'Could you order a cup of tea first?' she asked, smiling. Sudha was pleased that she had addressed her in the friendly second person singular and not in a more formal manner.

When the waiter came she ordered tea and, after asking Sandhyabai what she would like, asked for an onion rava dosa for her and a glass of pomegranate juice for herself.

'Let me pay for this,' said Sandhyabai.

'That's all right,' said Sudha and before the dosa and juice arrived, she told Sandhyabai about her detective agency and about herself in general.

A Meeting on the Andheri Overbridge

Sandhyabai listened to her, a bit amazed but silent.

The tea arrived first. Sandhyabai drank it slowly, blowing into the cup to cool it down.

'Are you a Madrasi?' Sandhyabai asked a little while later.

'Yes mausi, don't you like Madrasis?'

'Nothing like that. I just asked. *Tutsa Marathi changla aahe.* [Your Marathi is good.]' She then ate very quietly.

When she had finished eating, she drank another cup of tea and then, despite Sudha's entreaties, paid the bill.

They again got into the car and Sudha drove to her place. Once they arrived there, Sandhyabai looked around. Stella was sitting at the computer in the office. Sudha called out to Stella and introduced her.

There was still some time for Chellammal's arrival. Stella asked Sandhyabai to sit down and brought two glasses of cold water, placing them in front of her on the little stool. Sudha too sat down and in a soft voice asked her, 'Mausi, what is the problem? Can you tell me?'

'It is a very big problem, beti! A problem without a solution.'

'There is no problem without a solution. Please do tell me.'

Sandhyabai started speaking in a low voice.

Sandhyabai was from Karjat. Her father had been a farmer, her mother not just a farmer's wife. She hadn't hesitated to work beside her husband at the farm. She was capable of arguing and discussing everything about crops and sowing techniques with him. Sandhyabai was one of two sisters, Sandhyabai and Shantabai. Though they had both completed their schooling, they were used to working in mud and slush. They loved the soil deeply. When Sandhyabai got married she was twenty-two years old. It was a wedding arranged by her parents. The man they had chosen for her was a government employee in Mumbai. He had a pleasant, smiling face and a friendly disposition. His name was Prakash. Though she was excited and eager to go to Mumbai, she was also sad to leave her home town.

'Baba, ask him if he likes farming,' she said to her father.

Her soon-to-be husband had never ever been to a village. Mumbai was his home town. He had been born and brought up in Dadar. His mother, like any woman from Mumbai, walked with a quick and confident gait. She didn't wear a 'nauvari' sari of nine yards but wore a sari of six yards. His father did not wear a dhoti like Sandhyabai's father did, and wore trousers instead. Sandhya was rather frightened. But she learnt later that they were genuinely good people and, in the wadi where they lived, there was no one who did not look up to them.

In 1978, in the second year of their marriage, Mahesh was born. In 1980, Mangesh. In 1981, Prakash's parents passed away, one after the other. The house that they had been living in was not their own. It belonged to a distant relative. Only when the owner's son came to ask for it did they realize they should have bought a house themselves. The wadi was in Dadar; they did not think it would be possible for them to buy a house in the same locality. In Mumbai, it is not easy to buy in an area like Dadar. They began to look around in the Borivili area. They found two one-bedroom apartments adjacent to each other in a building constructed in 1978. Friends and relatives advised them to buy both. They said their two sons would have a place each in the future. Each apartment cost seventy-five thousand rupees. Prakash did not have the money. The medical expenses he had had to bear for his parents in their last days had drained his resources.

Sandhya's father came forward with half the amount required. For the remainder, Sandhya's jewellery was sold. They were the solid heavy gold jewellery that her aayi had given her. Both houses had been bought in Sandhya's name. Then they demolished the wall between the two flats and made it into one large house.

Sandhyabai paused for a little while.

Sudha felt that this was a story which ended

A Meeting on the Andheri Overbridge

with 'They got married and lived happily ever after'. Where was the problem in this? She looked at Stella. Stella slowly rose to make some cinnamon tea. She filled the electric kettle with water and switched it on.

~

Sandhyabai sat with her head bent, looking at her hands.

When Stella brought out a tray with teacups, Sandhyabai took a cup and wondered, 'Can one make tea with cinnamon?'

'This is what Sudha madam likes,' said Stella.

Sandhyabai began to sip the tea slowly.

Sudha began softly, 'Mausi, there seems to be no problem in all that you have told me until now.'

Sandhyabai did not reply but continued sipping her tea. Then she began to speak again.

The flats were bought, they moved in and the two sons grew up, studied and got jobs. Two lovely daughters-in-law, grandchildren...so far everything was cause for celebration. No harsh words, no fights, no disgust on faces, no bad moods.

Prakash had retired from work just two years ago. Savings in the bank, money from the provident fund – they had a tidy sum in their hands. When everything was going smoothly, her baba died. Aayi had passed away two years before that. Her sister Shantabai had gone back with her husband to the village and stayed with her baba after her aayi died. Shantabai's husband had taken a keen interest in farming.

Just a month before Sandhyabai's sixtieth birthday, Shantabai's husband died. Sandhyabai felt that her sixtieth birthday was a real turning point in her life.

Memories of her schooldays with her sister Shantabai, memories of the time when they used to sit on the wall of the well and gaze at their reflection in the water below, and of running to the fields as soon as they got back from school came back to her. She began having long conversations with her dead mother as she woke up in the morning. Her grandchildren would look at her in

A Meeting on the Andheri Overbridge

astonishment. But the real reason for her to take the decision that she took was the conversation that she had with Shantabai.

Every morning Shantabai would call her. That day when she called her voice sounded very low.

'What is it, Shanta?' Sandhyabai asked.

'Today it is going to be one month since Vinod passed away. Tai, I want to sleep with my head on your lap. I am not able to sleep at all. Vinod was a good man. He lived a good life and had a good death. But his was not an age to die. After all, he was the same age as you, wasn't he, tai?

'Tai, I have a thought in my mind. Maybe we will live for twenty more years. Can you not be with me for those twenty years? You and I can plant a herb garden in a corner of the fields. Yesterday I opened a cupboard in the inner room. There was an old box inside with an old notebook full of aayi's recipes for ragi dishes that she had written down for me. Ragi laddus, ragi halva, ragi mush, ragi dosa. Those are not just recipes, tai, it is their generation's secret for good health. Besides that there were many notes about herbs. Aayi and baba dreamt of planting a herb garden with medicinal plants and flowers on the other side of the well and harvesting it. All morning I just stayed there leaning against that cupboard, tai.'

As Shantabai spoke, Sandhyabai felt a very pleasant sensation down her spine. A kind of delight rose and filled her being. She imagined them both in their village home, working with many others, inside the house, outside, in the fields, eating ragi mush, growing jaswanti, sadaphuli, rose, jasmine – the next twenty years seemed like an endless expanse of green.

Aayi–baba's house, those old vessels, the corded cots, pots, brass utensils, dark green, dark blue and blood red nauvari saris, blouses with borders, the photographs taken at the weekly markets whenever they went there, all those came up as a precious museum gallery in her mind.

She did not even know when Shantabai disconnected the phone. She spoke about it to the others on her sixtieth birthday, which they were not celebrating as it had been only a month since Vinod had died.

'I am thinking of going to Karjat.'

Everyone was fine with the idea.

'Yes aayi, go and stay there for about two months or so. It'll be a comfort to mausi,' said Mangesh.

'Yes aayi, you must go,' his wife concurred.

Prakash never denied her anything she asked for. He too told her that she should go to Karjat and stay there for a month or two.

She listened to what everyone said and then said softly, 'Not two months. I have decided to go and live there forever.'

This shocked everyone.

'Sandhya, what do you mean? "I am going to stay there forever"? Don't I, your family and all this mean anything to you?' asked Prakash.

'You're a Mumbaikar. Will you like Karjat? I'll be happy if you come too. But you will be bored. You need the Mumbai local trains. You want the crowds. You want the seafront. You need your friends to go to Wankhede Stadium to watch cricket matches, watch Marathi plays, attend music concerts.'

'What about you? How will you be able to pass the time? How much can you talk to Shanta?'

'Shanta and I are going to plant a garden of herbs and flowers.'

Everyone burst into laughter.

'This is a time when farmers are drowning in debt and committing suicide, aayi. You cannot do this,' pronounced Mahesh.

His wife Leela was a college professor. 'Aayi, it is not uncommon to have this kind of strange idea at your age. I think you're tired of being in the house for so long. If you want, I'll take two weeks off. Why don't we all go somewhere, to Mahabaleshwar, Shirdi, Nashik?'

Sandhyabai softly refused her suggestion. 'It is not like that.'

'What is this herb-verb nonsense? Besides, can you move in with Shanta just like that? Don't we have to send you some money every month for expenses? Isn't that a waste of money?' Prakash raised his voice.

'I have already thought about that. Baba paid half the money to buy this house. The other half

A Meeting on the Andheri Overbridge

I gave by selling my jewellery. I asked an estate agent; he says now this house will fetch more than two crore rupees. We could divide that into five parts. The fifth part is to make up for all that Mahesh and Mangesh have spent so generously on the running of the house all these years. So three parts to the two of them. The fourth and fifth parts for the two of us. I'll take my share and go. Mahesh and Mangesh work in large corporate companies. They can get a bank loan and, using their share, they can buy flats wide as an ocean. What is the problem with that? Or if you want to continue living here, the two of you could buy me out. Your baba can stay with either one of you. He has enough money for his daily needs. He could come to Karjat. If he does, I'll be very happy.'

Everyone was shaken up.

Prakash came up to her and patting her on the back said, 'Sandhya, just go and sleep a little.'

'I am not sleepy.'

The next day their family doctor visited. He asked her a lot of questions. When she told him about the herbal plants he nodded at the others.

He said she needed total rest. A year passed but this sense of uncertainty lingered. Though she was in perfect health, she was dealt with like a pitiable creature and given love and compassionate treatment. The deeds to the house were deposited in the bank just to make sure she did not do anything without their knowledge.

When she learnt that they were trying to get a certificate from a psychiatrist to say that she was in a mentally confused state because of a delayed post-menopausal reaction that some women suffer, she decided to leave home.

'You could have gone to Karjat, mausi. Why should you go and sit in the Andheri station?'

'I won't go without collecting my share,' she said very firmly and clearly.

'By now they must have reported to the police that you're missing.'

'No. There is no one at home now. Mahesh and Mangesh have gone to Singapore for two weeks with their families. And Prakash has gone to Delhi on some work.'

'Then why did you leave the house? Why did

A Meeting on the Andheri Overbridge

you go and sit in Andheri station?' Sudha repeated her question.

'They had told the girl who works in our house to stay with me all day. They may have done it out of their love for me but it felt like it was done to keep an eye on me. I could not bear it. I went to Borivili station. I'd frequently travel to Andheri to shop and to go to the temple in the Seven Bungalows area. So I had a train pass. I got in very quickly when the train came. Only when I got down in Andheri, I found myself totally confused. Where can a sixty-year-old woman find a place to stay if she runs away from home? People will tell her to go to an ashram. So I just sat down in the station. I was weighed down by a large rock of sadness in my heart. I was being punished for expressing what I felt. If I had died without ever telling them, they would have made much of me. Sudha, do you believe in reincarnation? I don't. My baba used to say, hell and heaven are only in your heart. And only when you're alive. After we die, we're all air, just air.'

Sandhyabai's voice was quivering.

Sudha took both her hands and pressed them together and asked, 'Wouldn't that girl have phoned and told them by now?'

'No. I told her that I am going to a friend's place and would stay over for the night.'

'You have really been hasty in your decision, mausi.'

'No, Sudha. I was afraid that they would get that certificate as soon as they returned from their trips.'

'OK, let us see,' said Sudha, getting up.

Chellammal had come in and begun the cooking. The aroma of onions being fried filled the entire house.

~

Sudha asked Stella to continue talking with Sandhyabai and went in. She first dialled Mithra's number.

Mithra was at home. She had not left for the social service organization where she worked.

'Mithra, I saw a woman in Andheri station,' she

said and proceeded to give her the details. At once Mithra said, 'Her name is Sandhyabai, isn't it?'

'Yes.'

'She had come to us about a year ago. That is a complicated case, Sudha. We tried very hard to talk to her family. But they are adamant. They do not understand much of what she is saying. Why don't you try speaking to Lydia? Her organization will deal with it from the legal point of view.'

Next she contacted Lydia. 'In a case like this we have to adopt some sort of a drastic course. Otherwise it will drag on and on. You know Krupa Edward's story, don't you? We have to take exactly the same kind of steps we took in that case. That is the only way possible. Ask her if she agrees. After that, ask her about the deeds to the house, the receipt for selling the jewellery, the details of the cheque given by her father and so on. Anyway, what else? What news? How is your detective business faring?'

In Krupa's case they had all had to do their bit. Though Sudha had no connection with the case, she too had become part of it once Inspector

Shelke's help was sought. Krupa's husband had chased her out of the house with just the clothes she had on her. Krupa taught at a college. The girl students just adored her. So did the boys. That is what the husband could not stand. He kept their son with him and drove her out with their ten-year-old daughter. A friend of hers who had gone abroad had a place in Colaba. She spoke to her and got the key to the house from someone and went there. It was an empty house. Then she got in touch with Lydia. Lydia and Mithra got in touch with Shelke through Sudha and they discussed the issue. The sofa, the refrigerator, the TV, the bed and the table were all given to her as part of her dowry – all the fruits of years of hard work by her widowed mother, who had been a schoolteacher. The son, whom the husband had kept with him, could not manage without his mother.

It took them just one day's planning.

In the morning when they went to the son's school and met him with the principal's permission, his cheek bore the red imprint of somebody's palm. 'Appa was drunk and he slapped

A Meeting on the Andheri Overbridge

me,' he said, his voice choking up. They took him straight to the police and registered a complaint. They also told him to come to the Colaba house after school.

Next they went to Krupa's house with a lorry. Her husband had gone to his office. Krupa had a key. None of them picked up the phone when it kept ringing. The furniture, the TV, the refrigerator, the kitchen stuff, jewellery, bank account books, clothes - everything was loaded on to the truck and taken to the Colaba house within the hour. When the son came back from school, the Colaba house was all set up.

Sandhyabai's story was different. It would have to be approached in an entirely different manner. With the notes that Stella had made on the notepad as she was speaking to Sandhyabai, Sudha called Govind Shelke.

'Govind, are you very busy?'

'Never too busy for my didi.'

'Govind, it is a family problem.'

'In your family? Shall I come and fight with Naren bhaisaheb?' he said with a laugh.

'Does family mean only my family?' she asked and then explained everything.

'Hmm,' he said.

'Is there any way, Govind?'

'There is no straightforward way.'

'Then?'

'Didi, let mausi go home. We should make sure that the girl who does the housework does not come for a week. What did you say her name was?'

She referred to the notes and said, 'Manda.'

'Where does she live? Close by?'

'Ganesh Nagar.'

'Single woman?'

'No, her husband is an autorickshaw driver. They've three children. I believe she is a very good woman.'

'OK, is the bank account in mausi's husband's name or is it a joint account?'

'It's a joint account.'

'Where are the deeds to the house?'

'In the bank locker, of course.'

'Right. Would it be possible for me to speak to her?'

A Meeting on the Andheri Overbridge

'I'll just get her.' She asked Sandhyabai to come to the phone.

Sandhyabai listened very carefully to everything Govind Shelke said. After the conversation ended she said to Sudha, 'What he says is correct.'

Though she agreed to go back home and also to the other parts of the plan, there was a kind of hesitation in Sandhyabai. As Chellammal laid the table for them, she asked Sudha, 'Sudhamma, shall I go and stay with her for a day or two? She does seem a bit upset.' When Sudha conveyed this to Sandhyabai, her face lit up and she said yes immediately.

After lunch, Sudha took them to Borivili in her car. On the way they picked up the suitcase from the hostel. They told Mary that they did not need the room for the next two days. They went to Chellammal's house and picked up some clothes for her stay with Sandhyabai.

By the time they reached Borivili it was three o'clock. Manda was delighted to see Sandhyabai and welcomed her. A Marathi serial was running on TV. She first brought a glass of water for everyone. Then hesitantly she said, 'Aaji, in our basti there is a person taking people to Shirdi and Nashik by minibus. It is someone's pledge to god to do this. Could I be given leave for a week?'

'One week?'

'There is some problem with Sunil's auto licence. After coming back from Shirdi I'll have to attend to that. Please, aaji!'

'OK, then go. This aunty will stay with me.'

The Shirdi trip was Shelke's machination, Sudha reckoned.

Manda left.

'Mausi, where is the bank locker key?' Sudha asked. Sandhyabai said it was in the cupboard inside.

'OK mausi, I'll come tomorrow around ten. Chellamma will stay with you meanwhile. She is like my sister. Actually she was the one who raised Aruna.'

For the first time, Sandhyabai smiled properly and her entire face lit up.

~

A Meeting on the Andheri Overbridge

The trip to the bank did not prove to be difficult at all. The deeds to the house were in a separate file in a locker in the bank. Through a manager who had worked for more than thirty years in another branch of the bank, Shelke had found someone via whom the other issues could be addressed. When they approached this person, he was able to get for them the details of the cheque that Sandhyabai's father had given in 1982 along with other details, and have them photocopied. When they returned they opened the drawer where the old bank books were carefully arranged and picked out two books for 1982. They put them in the file with the papers that they got from the bank.

Then a trip to Kalbadevi. They did not even know whether the same jewellery shop still existed. Once they entered Kalbadevi, Sandhyabai's thoughts went back to the day they had sold the jewellery.

'The rainy season had just ended. We brought the jewellery in a velvet string bag. We came by taxi from Dadar. It would have been impossible to bring it safely in the train, wouldn't it? We had left Mahesh and Mangesh with the neighbours. When we came to Agarwal Jewellery and the man began weighing the jewels, Prakash's face looked wilted. He felt that he was committing a sin of sorts. They gave a cheque for seventy-five thousand rupees, which was a very large sum in those days. That champakali necklace that my aayi gave me was itself worth about twenty thousand. It was a flowerbud necklace, a really heavy, solid piece. Once we got the cheque, we went to the Rajasthani place that was nearby and had some puri halva. And some moong dal pakoras with it. I still remember.'

Agarwal Jewellery had been expanded. When they went to the young man at the cash register, he said, 'Now we have computerized all our accounts, aunty. I was not even born in 1982,' and laughed. 'Daddy is not here now.' Then he thought for a while and said, 'I have a chacha. Would you like to meet him? No matter how many times we tell him not to, he carries on with the old Marwari practice of keeping everything tied up in pieces of orange cloth.' He then told one of the shop stewards to take them to the rear of the shop.

A Meeting on the Andheri Overbridge

There they climbed up a circular iron staircase which led them to a large, air-conditioned room. There were open steel shelves with files bound together with orange cloth and account books covered with red cloth and tied up with white string. In a corner of the room was an old man sitting on an easy chair. The shop assistant who came with them bent down and told him in his ear the reason they had come.

After glancing at them briefly he told the shop assistant to take out the second bundle of files from the top shelf of the rack in the corner. When it was brought to him, he opened it up slowly and carefully. Using his thick, wrinkled index finger he riffled through the papers in the files and found the right file. He then went to the entries for the month of October that the shop steward had told him about and started looking through the papers.

'What did you say your name was?'

'Sandhyabai Pawar.'

'Did we give the receipt in your name?'

'I don't remember. Could be in his. Prakash Pawar.'

The index finger kept riffling through the papers.

At last, 'Here it is, in your name,' he said and showed it to her.

It was a list of jewellery items.
- Putala
- Mungachi haar
- Gulsari
- Vajratik
- Belpan
- Mohan mala
- Surya haar
- Kolhapuri saaz
- Putli haar
- Champakali haar

He slowly removed it from the file and gave it to the shop steward.

'Make a xerox copy and give it to them. Then bring it back here.'

The shop assistant took it and left.

The old man looked steadily at Sandhyabai.

A Meeting on the Andheri Overbridge

Then turning and looking out of the window at his side, he said softly,

'Chal jaag musafir bhor bhai
Ab rain kahan jo sowat hai.'

And then turning towards them he said, 'This is a bhajan. It could even be Kabir's.'

Then he explained, 'He says, "OK, get up, traveller, this is no time to sleep." Then he continues,

"Jo kal karna woh aaj karle
Jo aaj kare woh ab kare."

'He says, "What you have to do tomorrow, do it today, what you have to do today, do it now." Isn't that right?

'Listen to the next one:

"Jab chidiya ne chuk khet liya
Phir pachtaye kya hovat hai."

'After the sparrows have eaten up the entire field, what is the point of worrying, isn't it?'

By then the shop assistant had come back with a copy of the receipt. He deferentially handed the originals to the old man and then put back the paper in the file, tied it up properly and placed it in the same spot on the top shelf as instructed.

A boy brought three cups of tea. Masala chai it was.

The old man himself handed the cups to them.

He told Sandhyabai, 'Everything will work out fine,' as if he was an astrologer predicting the future.

When Sandhyabai briefly told him why it was important to obtain this receipt, he said, 'In matters of property, there are only two ways. One, you pin them down by sitting on their chest and get what you want. Or two, you give up. Your name is Sandhya, one of the 108 names of Durga. You should get on your lion, why don't you?' he said and laughed.

When they came out, they ate at the Rajasthani restaurant that was still in the same place. It still

A Meeting on the Andheri Overbridge

served puri halva as well as moong dal pakoras. They also ordered potatoes cut into small pieces and fried to a crisp as well as pickles. As they ate with relish they chatted away and Sandhyabai remembered her jewellery list.

'So many types of jewellery in those days! Do you know what a putala is? It is a necklace made of black and gold cords knotted with rows of gold coins. A gulsari is a choker made of a single thick gold chain. A thushi is also a choker, a large choker that aayi had given to Shantu. A Kolhapuri saaz is a necklace with several little pendants threaded on to it. It has twenty-one pendants of which ten depict the dasavathara of Vishnu, and eight depict the ashta mangalas of Lakshmi, and then two large red and green pendants, and then one very large pendant which we call a torala. It is to ward off all evil powers. All the other necklaces had five or six strands each with shapes of leaves and grains. Kolhapur is known for its jewellery. Aaji had given aayi a great deal of jewellery. Shantu was given the same amount of jewellery as me but with different designs. A cummerbund was given to her. That is to be worn around the waist. She had to sell all that to finance the children's education abroad. When she sold them, she got twenty lakh.'

As they were eating, Shelke called.

DSP Joseph Pinto's brother was thinking of buying a house in Borivili. He was an industrialist and he wanted to buy it for one of his companies. He said that he would give an advance and pay up the entire amount once the house was in his hands. He said he would be willing to wait for a month for them to vacate it. Or the house could be mortgaged and the money that was due to Sandhyabai could be taken. When the family came back, they could pay that sum and get the house back or think about selling it. If Sandhyabai felt that was the right way he would get the necessary papers organized and also bring a lawyer with him. This was the sum of the conversation with Shelke.

Sandhyabai went to wash her hands and when she returned she ate some of the candied fennel seeds that were in a bowl on the table. She stopped Sudha when she opened her purse to pay the bill and paid it herself.

When they sat in the car, Sudha said, 'Shall we do what Shelke says, mausi?'

'Yes. I feel that mortgaging it would be the best. Let them decide about selling the house. If they sell, that is fine; if they want to get it back by paying, that too is fine. That is their choice to make.'

She drove the car to Dr Manorama Mehta's house. Dr Mehta, a psychiatrist, was Sudha's friend. She had her clinic in her house. After speaking to Sandhyabai for a long time, she issued a certificate that said she was in good mental health.

When they went back home, Chellammal greeted them with a smiling face. Once they walked in she told Sandhyabai in Hindi, 'The phone rang twice. I did not pick it up.'

Sandhyabai remembered that she had put her phone in silent mode. She took it out and dialled her husband's number and talked to him. She told him that everything was fine.

Chellammal made tea with ginger and tulsi. She served everyone and, taking a cup for herself, she sat down with them. The conversation veered to personal matters and everyone talked about their own lives.

In the evening John Pinto came with his lawyer. Sandhyabai showed him the papers and said they were going to mortgage for the time being and the rest would depend on the wishes of the family. He accepted that. He liked the house and the price was right and he did wish to buy it. There was no question of 60 per cent white and 40 per cent black money as happens in all Mumbai transactions; he was in total agreement about paying 100 per cent white money by cheque. But he respected Sandhyabai's feelings and agreed to a mortgage. He also made a concession that he would not take interest from them for the month that Sandhya's family would take to make up their minds. He said that he did this in deference to Inspector Shelke's request since the inspector was held in high regard by Pinto's brother.

Sandhyabai signed the papers prepared by the lawyer and made another request to John Pinto. She had asked for two shares of the worth of the

A Meeting on the Andheri Overbridge

house divided into five parts as the money against the mortgage. Could she be given one share of it as a cheque and the other share as a direct transfer to a bank account? That was for her husband. The other three shares were for her sons and she asked the lawyer if he could prepare a legal document or a will to that effect.

John Pinto laughed. I can see that she is worried about her husband, he said. After the lawyer had done everything he needed to do, John Pinto stood up, bowed down low and gave her the cheque. He said he would also make the bank transfer of the money immediately.

Chellammal went in and brought out some payasam for everyone. No one knew when she had gone in to make it. The payasam was sweet with the taste of nutmeg and cardamom.

~

Sandhyabai packed all her belongings into two suitcases. They had arranged a rented van to take her to Karjat. The plan was that Sudha,

Chellammal, Sudha's daughter Aruna and Stella would all go with her.

The night before their journey, Sandhya showed Sudha the letter that she had written in Marathi to her husband. When Sudha hesitated to read it, she said, 'This is no simple letter, Sudha. This contains the notes of a life. I wish to share this with all of you. Please read it.'

'I speak Marathi well but I cannot read very well, mausi.'

'OK, then I'll read it,' Sandhya said.

Everyone sat around her. When she started reading, Aruna asked, 'Mausi, do you address your husband in the second person singular form?'

'Yes, when we're alone and when I write to him, that is how I address him. That's what he likes. Me too.'

She started reading afresh the letter in which her husband had been addressed in the familiar form.

My beloved friend Prakash,
   One monsoon season we got into a train from Karjat to come to Mumbai. All through the journey,

A Meeting on the Andheri Overbridge

there were waterfalls that looked like cascades of pure milk, the farms and trees a sea of green. Without worrying about your aayi and baba who were sitting facing us, you put your arm on my shoulder and said, 'I'll always be by your side.' You have kept your word for the past thirty-eight years. My love for you only keeps increasing every day. You're an amazing human being. I am an ordinary woman. I believed that as long as I had your shoulder to lean on, I would not need anything else. But all the while there was this other desire within me. My longing for the soil. I wanted to tell you that soon after you retired. But when Shantu asked me to come live with her in the village, that desire grew into a large tree and touched the sky.

Can I not live for myself? Is it a mental disorder to think so? I have cooked long enough. I have done enough for the family. Raised the children, celebrated festivals, made the required dishes for each of those, looked after the household accounts, helped with the childbirths and then all the nurturing that follows; all that I did with my whole heart with no complaints. You too have never faulted me for anything. I did not keep anything for myself. There was never any need to, either. But now I wish to embark on another path. An untravelled path. A sixty-year-old woman's journey is going to start. The path is a rough one, true. I could even fall. But I'll get up. I'll rise and walk again.

In my mind's eye I see a herb garden spreading out. Jaswanti and sadaphuli as well as roses and jasmine in bloom. Shantu stands beside me.

I have mortgaged this house and taken the share due to the two of us. In our bank account lies your share. All the papers are with this letter. Our sons and our daughters-in-law are as good as gold. They respect us. They love us. Tell them, aayi did this with full cognizance and with no anger and no grievances against them. For a woman to choose a unique path, does she need to be angry or sorrowful? Even if she is satisfied, happy and peaceful, can she not have dreams and the desire to fulfil them?

All my belongings that I require for my life have fitted into two boxes. There is nothing excessive in it. However, in a rose-coloured jewellery box there is a Lakshmi haar necklace which was your first present to me. You bought it for me on the first anniversary of our marriage. There were many nights when I only had the Lakshmi haar on as I lay next to you. What nights those were! That is why I am taking it with me. My love for you will never decrease, never dry up.

Do you remember that Kabir song, the one that Kumar Gandharva has sung? 'Ud jayega hans akela...'

The swan will fly away all alone
This world is but the spectacle of a market-fair
When the leaf falls from the tree
Who knows where it will fall
When a gust of wind strikes it?
The swan will fly away all alone

This swan has begun its flight. With only an endless sky for company.
Your Sandhya

When she finished reading there was complete silence.

Stella and Aruna, their eyes moist, got up slowly and went and hugged her from either side. Sandhyabai sat between them like a regal bird.

A Note on the Author

Ambai writes about love, relationships, quests and journeys with verve and compassion. This acclaimed Tamil writer brings a similar balance of brio and sympathy to the stories of her crime-solving protagonist, Sudha Gupta.

A Note on the Translator

Gita Subramanian has four published translations of Tamil novels to her credit. In 2010 she won the Nalli Thisai Ettum award for the best Tamil to English translation of the year.

Coming soon...

KANHAIYA KUMAR
BIHAR TO TIHAR

MY POLITICAL JOURNEY

A sneak peek into
Bihar to Tihar

My first tutor was Parmanand Yadav and it was he who taught me how to read in English. He would teach for about twelve or thirteen hours each day covering the entire locality. Of all his students I was the worst off. Some of his students were from homes with a car, TV and telephone but these were just a handful.

At the end of every month he gave a test to all his students, and soon I started to top them, just as I always topped the exams at my government school. This only added to Pitaji's problems. Pleased with my performance, Parmanandji began to put pressure on my father that I be taken out of my current school and put in a private school.

The year was 1996. Our education system had been undergoing a long period of transition. Privatization had become the new buzzword and the Education Policy of 1986 had begun to be implemented. This had sown the seeds of privatization. It was one of the first moves towards a new liberalization where the public sector was wilfully destroyed.

Prior to this, a large number of states had mostly government schools, and despite being from different economic backgrounds, children studied in the same school. However, it wasn't as though all government schools fell under the same category. Those from less privileged homes studied in the middle and high schools of the state government while others from more prosperous backgrounds went to Kendriya Vidyalayas and could afford extra tuition.

Children of service-class parents easily got admission to these schools and sometimes children from their extended families were also passed off as their own and got into them. Above the Kendriya Vidyalayas stood the Netahat Sainik Schools or Jawahar Navodaya Vidyalayas which had been designed for the brightest students. This was a highly competitive school and very hard to get into. I must add here that the government school I studied in produced many students who went on to be very successful in different areas.

Parmanandji told my father that he should put me into a private school and that he would simultaneously prepare me for the Jawahar Navodaya Vidyalaya. I bought an enormous work book to help me prepare to get into the school. It occupied more space than any of my other books.

Pitaji decided to follow my tutor's advice. I joined a private school called Sunrise Public School, aware that my family was sacrificing a lot to enrol me there. My private school fees were forty rupees per month and Parmanandji's fees were twenty-five rupees per month. Then there was the expense of school uniform and books. The school was three kilometres away and since I couldn't walk that distance every day, money was also arranged for the school rickshaw, an additional sixty rupees.

Sunrise Public School unfolded new social layers for me. When I studied in the government school I didn't understand class distinctions. There was no uniform and everyone wore their own clothes to school. In the private school there was a prescribed uniform. When people say uniforms camouflage social class they've got it all wrong. Actually it's the uniform that gives away class. No matter what children wear to school by the end of the day it's dirty. Only those who have several sets of clothes can be in clean clothes every day. I had only one set of my uniform. By Friday it was filthy and sometimes actually stinking. Ma didn't realize this. In our family I was the first to go to a private school so no one in my family knew the dos and don'ts.

In the government school the books were in Hindi. In those days, Ma taught me every day while she cooked meals. But in the new school she couldn't do this anymore. There was a school diary, homework, classwork, separate copies, etc., and other than Hindi and Sanskrit all these books were in English.

This created an unpleasant distancing in the mother-son relationship. I started telling Ma things like 'What do you know? You don't know anything. You've only studied in a government school I'm in a private school', and so on. I also became aggressive towards my brothers and started showing off my knowledge of English. Ma never punished me, Pitaji was never home, and the entire neighbourhood looked up to me. I became very arrogant.

But while I could boss over Ma and bully the kids of my area, I couldn't lord over the children at my school. The class divide there left me isolated. Most of the kids had nice clothes, shoes, and several pairs of socks. They all looked clean. Most of them wore trousers, locally referred to as 'full pant'. Poor kids like me wore shorts, that is, 'half pant', to school. It was in class ten that I wore full pants for the first time in my life as part of the uniform given out by the government high school.

Each day, there was something or the other in the private school that separated me from the others. Very young children wore mufflers, which were quite expensive. Only those people who could afford them or who had someone who could knit them one had mufflers. My mother knitted a cap for me and when I wore it to school for the first time the children took it off and began playing with it, throwing it up in the air like a ball. I felt thoroughly ashamed and regretted the fact that from being at the top of the pile in the government school I had been reduced to a nonentity.

For the first time I was face to face with all the hardships students from the weaker sections had to face. The children in my private school didn't just wear good clothes, they also had cars and motorcycles to commute. It was a different world altogether. Until now I hadn't even been really familiar with my entire village; my knowledge was limited to my locality. But now I began to learn about the whole village. I had started sensing the difference between children living in kuchcha houses and pukka houses. I had started measuring time by the speed of the cars on the road. Difference and discrimination became part of my psyche.

Those early days set the pace for the experiences of the future. I already felt embarrassed about the low financial status of my family. Soon I began to lose my confidence about the one thing I had always been sure of: my studies. In my second day at the new school, I was slapped for the first time in life. The English teacher had asked me to stand up and read. The lesson was 'The Real Princess'.

While reading I got stuck at one point and the teacher beat me up.

The third source of embarrassment was to do with my understanding of the cultural norms of the new school. At the old one I read out poetry and sang and was among the best to do so. In the fine arts class, the teacher asked each child to sing a song. To make up for what had happened in the English class I was the first to raise my hand. I started singing a patriotic film song – *'Mera rang de basanti chola, maa ye, rang de basanti chola.'*

The entire class burst into amused laughter.

Madam said, 'What kind of a silly song is this? Go and sit down.'

The next boy sang *'Na kajre ki dhaar, na motiyon ka haar'*, a popular song from the film *Mohra*. Madam was very happy, while I was shocked. Till then I had believed that singing film songs in school was inappropriate.

It was hard for me to get my bearings. It was fine to sing *'Na kajre ki dhaar, na motiyon ka haar'* in the fine arts class. But boys and girls (who sat in different sections of the class) talking to each other was not fine, and was made fun of.

This mix of orthodox thinking and modernity in my new school was far more complex than the environment of my middle-class rural family and my government school.

It took me more than a year to get over my personal inadequacies. My cap and half pant remained unchanged, but I began to slowly make up by doing well in studies, as well as in literary and cultural activities. But that first year proved to be a tough one. That year for the Founder's Day celebrations on 12 December I was not selected for any event, not for singing or for public speaking.

What really upset me was my academic performance. I went to school to get my result, full of expectation. Half the exhilaration lay in carrying an empty bag to school since we didn't have to study on the day of the result. Each day I would trudge to school with a heavy bag full of books and the weightlessness on the big day added to my nervous excitement. But when I heard the result I was totally deflated. I was expecting to be among the top three but for the first time I had stood fifth in class. I went home with my report card.

When I reached home, Ma was washing clothes. That morning on my way to school I had had a little tiff with her. I was putting on my uniform without taking a bath and Ma got angry saying I didn't value the hard work put in by others. I should be clean when I wore my uniform because it took effort and money to keep it clean, even expensive fabric whitener had to be used. We, the poor, couldn't afford '*aaya naya Ujala char boondon wala*', that expensive brand of whitener. We bought loose indigo which had to be used carefully or it made clothes blotchy. All this was a great effort for Ma.

Bhaiya called out from a distance, 'Kanhaiyaji, where are you? It's time. We're getting late.' As I was leaving I heard mother say behind me, 'Walking away unbathed and unwashed…trying to be a dandy…'

My cocky behaviour would pain Ma greatly and our fight that day was especially sore. When I returned with the report card she asked, 'So, what is it?' Till today I haven't forgotten her tone, the underlying bitter humour in the query. And as long as I remember it, my feet will stay on the ground – family is the first school and one's mother is the first teacher.

Ma was apprehensive that the change in my personality would not have a positive effect on my studies. All said and done, she was a unique woman who was taking care of the family, bringing up her children, and with her face covered under a *ghoonghat*, also going to school herself. She understood the importance of education.

With a heavy heart I said, 'Fifth.'

'You're saying "fifth" as though you've topped.'

I had no answer. Ma told me that now I knew where I really stood. 'Earlier you were in a government school where there was hardly any teaching anyway. Now in a private school you've come to know your place.'

Her words were a big blow to me. The next year, no one scored as high as I did. But I only learnt of it much later. The previous year's result had left such a scar that I didn't go to find out how I'd done. Earlier too, I had never been interested in finding out the result but that was because it was understood that I would be first. Now I just didn't have the guts.

Ma didn't ask about the result. Those days Pitaji used to go to Kodarma (then in Bihar, now in Jharkhand) to buy rubble, which he then sold in the local market. This kept him away for several days at a stretch. When he returned, Pitaji asked about the result. I told him that I hadn't gone to get it. Pitaji borrowed a bike from someone and took me to school. The school was closed but the principal, Ramkumarji, was in office. Seeing me he said warmly, 'Come, Kanhaiya, come.' Seeing his warmth made me even more frightened.

But Pitaji came to my rescue. Steering the conversation in another direction he said that he hadn't been able to pay the fees for the last few months and so had come now to settle it. The fees were paid and the principal himself wrote out the receipt. Though this was a private school which tried to ape its urban counterparts, the resources here were limited. Private schools in villages were not that different from government schools – they simply had the word 'convent' or 'public school' in their name.

As we were leaving Pitaji brought up the real issue. He said he wanted to know my result. Seeing the principal's eyes light up made me go cold all over again. He told us I had got an 'A' grade. This didn't ring a bell with my family; they were more familiar with the roll number system. The principal explained that my roll number was three but in this school that was not important. I had topped my class.

Even in December's annual celebrations that year, I was at the top. There was no event in which I did not participate – singing, public speaking, acting, writing…I was everywhere.

The results went a long way in raising my self-esteem. My English too had improved over the year. Parmanandji no longer had the time, and in any case it was difficult for him to help me with the syllabus of Sunrise. So he found another teacher for me. Things were slowly beginning to look good.

juggernaut

THE APP FOR INDIAN READERS

Fresh, original books tailored for mobile and for India. Starting at ₹10.

juggernaut.in

1

CRAFTED FOR MOBILE READING

Thought you would never read a book on mobile? Let us prove you wrong.

juggernaut.in

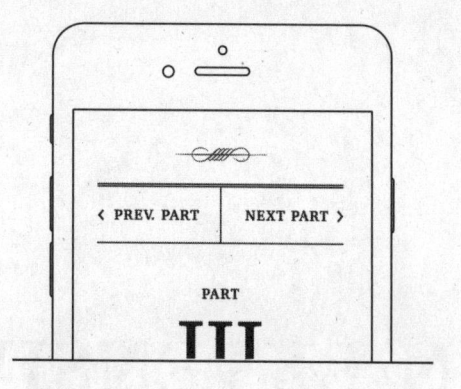

Beautiful Typography

The quality of print transferred to your mobile. Forget ugly PDFs.

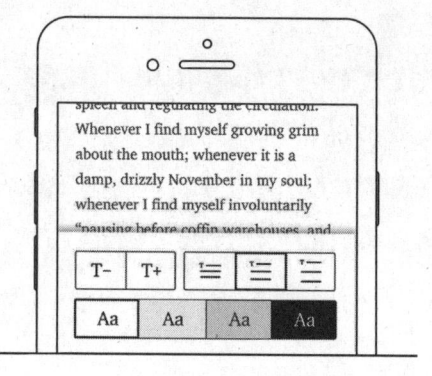

Customizable Reading

Read in the font size, spacing and background of your liking.

juggernaut.in

AN EXTENSIVE LIBRARY

Including fresh, new, original Juggernaut books from the likes of Sunny Leone, Praveen Swami, Husain Haqqani, Umera Ahmed, Rujuta Diwekar and lots more. Plus, books from partner publishers and loads of free classics. Whichever genre you like, there's a book waiting for you.

juggernaut.in

juggernaut.in

3

DON'T JUST READ; INTERACT

We're changing the reading experience from passive to active.

juggernaut.in

Ask authors questions

Get all your answers from the horse's mouth. Juggernaut authors actually reply to every question they can.

Rate and review

Let everyone know of your favourite reads or critique the finer points of a book – you will be heard in a community of like-minded readers.

Gift books to friends

For a book-lover, there's no nicer gift than a book personally picked. You can even do it anonymously if you like.

Enjoy new book formats

Discover serials released in parts over time, picture books including comics, and story-bundles at discounted rates. And coming soon, audiobooks.

juggernaut.in

4

LOWEST PRICES & ONE-TAP BUYING

Books start at ₹10 with regular discounts and free previews.

juggernaut.in

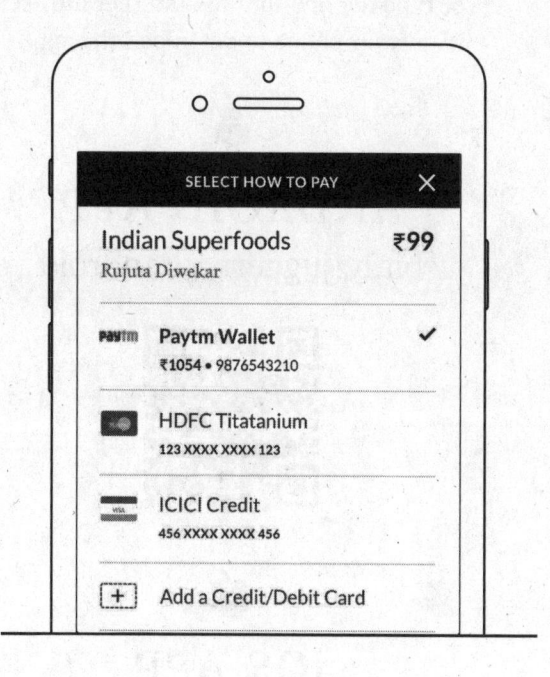

Paytm Wallet, Cards & Apple Payments

On Android, just add a Paytm Wallet once and buy any book with one tap. On iOS, pay with one tap with your iTunes-linked debit/credit card.

Click the QR Code with a QR scanner app or type the link into the Internet browser on your phone to download the app.

ANDROID APP
bit.ly/juggernautandroid

iOS APP
bit.ly/juggernautios

For our complete catalogue, visit www.juggernaut.in
To submit your book, send a synopsis and two sample chapters to books@juggernaut.in
For all other queries, write to contact@juggernaut.in